Heart of the Damned

Georgina Stancer

To Therena

Thank you for being
an active member
of the group
much love
Georgine Stancer

Editing by Stacey Jaine McIntosh
Cover design by EmCat & Butterfly Designs

www.georginastancer.co.uk

This book is dedicated to my sister Heather.

No matter how many miles have separated us, she has always been there for me, and I know she always will be. I don't tell her this often enough, but she is the best sister in the entire world.

Contents

Prologue

"Quickly, Amberly," her mother urged as she pulled her along behind her. "You've got to be faster."

"I'm trying," Amberly said between panting breaths.

Her little legs weren't able to go as fast as her mother's yet, but she was getting faster every day. She was even practising in the bunker so she could keep up the next time they needed to move.

Unfortunately, she still wasn't fast enough. No matter how much she practised, her legs just weren't long enough. She always ended up falling behind, making her mother slower because of her.

"It's not much further," her mother promised.

Amberly didn't reply, she was finding it hard to breathe let alone speak.

"Here!" a woman shouted from up ahead. "We're

over here!"

Amberly's mother suddenly swept her off her feet and ran in the direction the woman had shouted from.

"Take her," her mother said, handing Amberly over to the woman as soon as they reached her.

"Come inside quickly," the woman said.

"I can't," her mother said, shaking her head. "They're right behind us. I've got to lead them away."

She gently brushed the hair out of Amberly's face and kissed her on the forehead before racing off into the woods.

"Mummy!" Amberly shouted.

"Shh, little one, they'll hear you," the woman whispered in her ear.

"But my Mummy," Amberly whimpered.

"I know, little one, I know," the woman softly crooned as she carried Amberly down the ladder and deeper into the bunker.

***

"Amberly," Donovan called her name as he gently shook her awake. "Amberly, you're having a nightmare again."

"I'm awake," she groaned.

If only it was just a nightmare, she would be able to handle it, but it wasn't. It was a memory from her childhood, one she would much rather forget.

She wanted to remember the good times with her mother. She might only have a few of them, but she was trying desperately to hold on to them. She didn't want her main memory of her mother to be the last time she saw her.

Anything was better than that one.

"Thanks for waking me," she told him.

It wasn't the first time Donovan had interrupted her dreams, and it probably wouldn't be the last either. As much as she missed her mother and wanted to see her in her dreams, she was grateful each and every time he woke her up.

"No problem," he said.

"Has the storm eased off any yet?" she asked.

They were halfway through a mountain pass when a horrendous snowstorm hit. It came out of nowhere, rolling over the mountain peaks and encasing them in a wall of white, like a wave crashing over them.

Within seconds, they couldn't see a thing. So, they had no choice but to take shelter in the nearest cave. Thankfully, there were plenty of caves about for them to choose from.

When they first set out along the mountain pass the weather had been fine, but it soon turned against them. Admittedly, they should have known it might happen. They should have prepared for it. After all, mountains were extremely unpredictable.

Amberly couldn't stop her thoughts from drifting to Natalia. Not long after they'd set off, her best friend had turned back to go looking for another member of their group.

Bella had wondered off, most likely in a tantrum. She

was prone to throwing a hissy fit whenever she didn't get her own way, which was the majority of the time.

Most of the group thought it was because they'd left people behind when they left the last bunker, but Amberly disagreed. She had a feeling Bella stormed off because she didn't like the fact that Natalia was in charge.

She'd always had a superiority complex. Butting heads with Natalia at every opportunity she got. Even though none of them liked the woman, they couldn't leave her behind, but especially not Natalia.

After the last of the elders had gone, Natalia took on the leadership role since nobody else stepped up to the plate. Nobody wanted the responsibility of making sure everyone in the group was safe, which was a difficult task when there were literally thousands of monsters out to kill them.

With very few humans still alive, it was imperative to keep everyone safe, even if they were the biggest dick in the world.

"Yeah, it's eased off quite a bit," Donovan said. "We should be able to carry on when you're ready."

"Good," she said. "We need to reach the other side before another one hits. I don't know how much further our supplies are going to stretch. So, we can't risk being stuck here for too much longer."

They'd only packed enough to last them a few days. It should have been enough to last until they reached the other side, but they would need to look for more as soon as they arrived. If they're stuck in a cave for too many days, they were going to run out way before they made it.

Hopefully Natalia wasn't far behind them. She had even less supplies on her than they did.

"Make sure everyone is ready to go in ten," she said, stretching out her aching muscles.

The blanket she'd laid out on the floor did little to stop the cold from seeping into her skin. Her bones ached from sleeping on the cold hard rock. Well, what little sleep she managed to get.

"They're all ready to leave," he said. "We're just waiting for you."

"Oh, okay," she said. Sitting up with a groan, she wrapped the blanket around her legs and scooted closer to the fire. "Give me a minute to wake up properly first, and then we'll get going."

"No problem," he told her before standing up. "Take as long as you need."

He re-joined the others by the entrance to the cave, leaving her alone to wake up and get herself ready.

She didn't want to get up. As much as the cold hard ground made her bones ache, she knew it was going to be worse outside. Even if the storm had passed and all was calm, it was still freezing out there.

She watched as Donovan talked with the others. She appreciated his help keeping everyone together and safe while Natalia was looking for Bella.

Their group wasn't as big as it once was, but it was still bigger than she could handle on her own. She didn't envy Natalia's job. She would much rather support

Natalia than take her place.

Sometimes she wished she'd been born before the Great War, before all the monsters that went bump in the night came crawling out to take over the world. Back when life was simple and nothing was out to kill them.

Back then, nobody knew the monsters they read about in books were actually real. That all changed the day the war broke out. Every mythical and supernatural creature ever written about… and some that weren't… came out of hiding to fight one another.

The Human race was decimated over the course of the war. Caught up in the middle of a fight they had nothing to do with, they were unable to find somewhere safe to wait it out.

It wasn't until the war ended that the real problems started. No longer fighting amongst themselves, the monsters turned their attention solely on the Humans. Ever since then, they had hunted down and killed her kind nearly to extinction.

If it hadn't been for the secret bunkers dotted around, Amberly was certain there wouldn't be any Humans left. Thankfully, they were able to hide in the bunkers, but it was only a matter of time before the monsters cottoned on.

If Amberly was honest, she was surprised they hadn't cottoned on already.

Nobody knew why there were so many hidden bunkers scattered across the land, but they were grateful to whoever put them there. Without them, the Human race would have gone extinct years ago.

For all she knew, their group could be the last of their kind. Which was why Natalia hadn't wanted to leave Bella behind, no matter how annoying she was.

Before joining the others by the entrance to the cave, Amberly pulled out a few items from her bag and put them in a separate one. If she was right, Natalia was going to need extra provisions before reaching the other side.

She knew it was a long shot leaving a bag of food in the cave. There was no guarantee Natalia would stop there, but Amberly had to do something. She couldn't stay there and wait for Natalia, but she could leave a care package hoping she found it.

Climbing to her feet, she rolled up the blanket and stuffed it into her bag. Turning her attention to the fire, she kicked dirt over it to put it out. Instantly, the cold air wrapped itself around her.

Amberly pulled her coat tight around her. Throwing the bag over her shoulder, she traipsed to the entrance to join Donovan and the rest of the group.

"Right, I'm ready to go," she said as she walked up to them.

"Okay," Donovan said, clapping his hands. "Let's go everybody."

A few people moaned as they walked out into the freezing wind, pulling their coats tighter around them.

With one last look behind her at the bag, Amberly headed out the cave and followed the others as they made their way through the snow-covered mountain-pass.

Chapter 1

"Finally!" Donovan said. "I can see a bunker."

"Where is it?" Amberly asked.

Donovan instantly pointed out the rusty disc half buried by overgrown bushes.

None of the bunkers were easy to find, they wouldn't be very good hiding places if they were, but it was even harder when they didn't know the area. None of their group had been on this side of the mountain before, so none of them knew the lay of the land.

"Thank fuck for that," one of the other men in the group said.

"Wait here a minute while I check it out," Donovan told them.

"Okay," Amberly agreed.

Crouching down in the undergrowth, they all watched

as Donovan crept over to the manhole that hid the entrance to the bunker. He wasn't only making sure it was safe; he was making sure it was available.

It would be great to see other Humans still alive, but at the same time, it would be awkward joining up with another group. They'd been on their own for so long, it would be strange having more people around.

Donovan lifted the manhole and climbed inside. Amberly's heart was in her throat as she waited for him to reappear. It seemed to take forever.

When he finally poked his head up, he quickly waved them over.

"Hurry," he said.

Not wasting a second, they all jumped up and raced over. One by one, they quickly climbed down the ladder as soon as they reached him.

Amberly was the last one through the door. She made sure nobody was left outside before locking the door tightly behind them and descending into the dark bunker.

She prayed they hadn't been seen as they entered the bunker. The last thing they wanted was to be spotted entering or exiting any of the bunkers. The monsters would know they were hiding underground, so they would concentrate on tracking down the bunkers, and ultimately, the last of her kind.

Amberly didn't want to be the one that gave it away after so many years of keeping it secret. She was amazed the monsters still hadn't figured out they were living underground, but she wasn't complaining. It meant she was able to live, if that's what you call it.

Spending most of your life underground, and constantly being on the run, was no way to live. Never being able to play in the fields as a young girl. Never being able to just enjoy being out in the open, under the summer sun. Never being able to play in the autumn leaves, or have snowball fights.

That's how Amberly had lived her entire life. Hiding in bunkers underground while monsters roamed above, trying to kill her at every turn.

The only time she was allowed above ground was to look for food and other supplies, or move to a new bunker. It wasn't safe to stay in one area for too long, so they had no choice but to move around.

If it wasn't for the food and other essentials they scavenged from the monsters, they would have died out long ago. It was impossible to grow anything underground, and they couldn't keep livestock because there were creatures out there that could turn into any living creature. Humans found that out the hard way.

Amberly's mother told her stories when she was younger, and one of them was about Humans keeping some animals as pets. Dread always filled her when her mother said some of them turned out to be monsters all along.

For one reason or another, the monsters used to pretend to be innocent creatures and lived among Humans. Amberly couldn't wrap her mind around why they would live like that. How they could get close to Humans and then suddenly turn on them.

So nowadays, Humans didn't take the chance. They avoided all living creatures because they couldn't be certain what was real and what was not.

There weren't many of them left, so they couldn't risk losing any more people. Which was one of the reasons Natalia had gone back for Bella.

By the time she reached the main living quarters, lanterns had been lit and were dotted around the room.

Their new accommodation wasn't the largest place she'd stayed in, but they were safe, and that was the main thing. A safe place they could hole up while they waited for Natalia to catch up.

As soon as Natalia arrived, they could discuss what they were going to do next. Whether they were going to stay in the area, or move further away from the mountains.

Either way, they'd only be able to stay there for a short time before having to move on. She just hoped Natalia had caught up to them before that time came.

"It's freezing in here," one woman in the group complained as she pulled a blanket around her shoulders.

"It'll soon warm up," Amberly told her. "Once we've settled in and got a fire going, it'll be just like the last place."

Unfortunately, they had to wait until after dark before lighting the fire and only for a short time as well. Whatever heat they managed to get in that time would have to last them.

It was too risky to light a fire in the day. The smoke wasn't as noticeable at night as it was during the day.

So, any cooking that needed to be done had to be done after dark.

"Yeah, except for the fact we're down four people," one of the men said.

"There's nothing we can do about that," she said. "Hopefully Natalia will join us soon with Bella."

She didn't bother to bring up the other two people because it was highly unlikely that they would ever see them again. Not only had they moved bunkers, but they had travelled days away from the last one.

"If you think she's coming, then you're more naïve than I gave you credit," the man said. "We all know once you've left the group you don't return. It's not going to be any different for Natalia. No matter how much we all liked her, we all know we're never going to see her again."

"That's not true," Amberly said adamantly.

Even though he was right, she refused to believe she'd never see Natalia again.

"Go on then," he said mockingly. "How many people have come back to the group after they've left? And I'm not taking about just going out scavenging. I mean, literally leaving the group and meeting back up after you've moved to another bunker?"

"Don't give her shit," Donovan jumped to her defence. "She's only trying to stay positive for you lot. She didn't ask to be put in charge. Neither of us did, but here we are. We're doing our best."

"Nobody is denying that you're doing your best," the woman said. "We appreciate everything you do, but don't lie to us. We know the situation is worse than you're letting on. If we carry on losing people at the rate we have been, all too soon there's not going to be any of us left."

"I promise Natalia is returning," Amberly said. "I can't promise she'll have Bella with her, but I know she'll do whatever she can to bring her back as well."

"Nobody doubts that," the woman said.

"What do you doubt then?" Donovan asked. "Because it certainly sounds like it to me."

"We just don't want to be lied to," the woman said.

"When did we lie to you?" he asked.

"For one," the man said. "When you told us it was going to be better on this side of the mountain. From the looks of it so far, things are going to be a lot harder than they were before."

"Nobody promised it was going to be better," Donovan said. "If I remember correctly, you were all told that we didn't know what it was going to be like on this side of the mountain, because none of us have been here before. We took a vote, and you all voted to give it a try. So, don't turn around now and say that we lied to you, or hid the truth from you because you knew from the beginning that it was a long shot."

"Until we've had time to explore the area, we're not going to know if it was a good decision or not," Amberly said. "So, there's no point saying we're in a worse situation because we just don't know yet. For all we know, it could be the best decision we've ever made."

"I can't see that being the case," the man said. "I don't

know about you lot, but I didn't see any sign of life on our way here. I would think we would have seen something by now. It's not as if the bunker was right next to the mountains. We've covered more ground on this side than we did to get to the mountain from the last bunker."

"That may be so, but it doesn't mean there's nobody living this side," Donovan said.

"I haven't seen anything either," another woman said. "And I was looking for tracks."

"Please," Amberly said. "Can we just get settled in first, and then we can figure out what to do next."

It wasn't as if they could go anywhere at the moment anyway. It was getting dark outside, which was the most dangerous time to be travelling.

Not only that, but Amberly was absolutely shattered, freezing cold, and starving. There was no way she was leaving the bunker and searching for another one until at least tomorrow.

She didn't even want to go outside for firewood, but somebody had to do it.

"We're not going anywhere tonight," Donovan said, reading her mind. "So, you might as well get settled in for the night."

There was a lot of moaning from everyone, but none of them said another word about it.

"Thank you," Amberly whispered to Donovan when the rest of the group moved away to look around the new bunker.

"No problem," he said.

He kissed her on the forehead before taking his bag through to the sleeping area.

Amberly missed Natalia. She would have known how to reassure everyone that it would all be okay in the end.

Unfortunately, Natalia wasn't there. And as much as Amberly told everyone that she would be back, she didn't know for sure.

They were right, once somebody left the group, they never returned. Especially not once they'd moved as well.

Amberly used to tell herself that the people who left the group had joined another one and were living happily somewhere. But in truth, they were more likely to be dead. It was a hard, brutal world they lived in, but it was the only one they had.

They could either learn to live with it, or they might as well just hand themselves over to the monsters. It would save a hell of a lot of time and resources, not that she would say that to anyone though.

Right, get your shit together girl, you've got work to do, she told herself sternly.

She didn't have time to mope around feeling sorry for herself. She had to keep things together until Natalia came back. She needed to pull up her big girl pants and get shit done.

Amberly had no right asking everyone else to have faith that everything was going to work out fine if she didn't have any herself.

Chapter 2

A couple of days off, was that too much to ask for? Dain didn't think so, but apparently it was.

Don't get him wrong, he enjoyed his job, but who wouldn't? He got to spend all of his time with his two best friends as they hunted down Humans, and he was good at it. But occasionally, he wanted a break from it all.

It wouldn't be so bad if they weren't killing the Humans they caught, or worse, selling them on to traders. He'd quite happily let them live if it was up to him. Unfortunately, if he didn't do it, somebody else would.

At least with him it was a quick and clean kill. With anyone else, it wasn't just a possibility; inevitably it would be a long drawn out death.

Dain had seen for himself what some Humans were

put through, and he wouldn't wish it on his worst enemy. The Humans were far from his worst enemy. They certainly didn't deserve the treatment they were given.

The females of the species had it worse off. More often than not, they were raped before being tortured and killed.

It was rare, but not unheard of for the males to suffer the same fate. They were tortured just like the females, but they were generally made to watch as their females were raped instead of it happening to them.

Either way, it was wrong and nobody deserved to go through it.

So, as Dain saw it, he was doing them a favour by hunting them down and killing them first. It was far better than the alternative.

Back when he first started hunting them, he thought exactly the same as everyone else. That the Humans were a disease, slowly destroying everything around them, and that they needed to be stopped.

Yes, they needed to stop destroying the planet, but they didn't need to be completely wiped from the world. They could learn to treat it with respect. At the least, they could have been given the chance to change.

Between fighting amongst themselves and hunting other species to extinction, the Humans were slowly poisoning the planet they lived on. If a war hadn't broken out between the supernatural species, exposing them all to the Humans, things might never have changed. But it did.

After the war ended, the supernatural beings turned

their attention on the Humans. Hunting them down and slaughtering them to near extinction in a bid to save the planet, and Dain had helped lead the charge against them.

All that was about to change though, and it was all because of a simple bet between his friends and hunting buddies, Arun and Taredd. A simple bet to see who the better hunter was out of the two of them.

Dain wasn't part of the bet because they already knew he was the best hunter out of the three of them. One of the many perks to being a Shapeshifter was being able to use the senses of any animal, great or small.

He slammed his empty glass on the counter and indicated that he wanted it refilling by the bartender. A moment later, his glass was half-full again.

Swirling the golden liquid around in the glass, he stared into thin air. His mind was ablaze with everything that had happened since their band of three separated a couple of days ago at the start of the bet.

All Dain had wanted was a couple of days off to recharge his batteries. Taredd, on the other hand, had wanted to carry on hunting down the Humans. Arun seemed to be with him, wanting time off. But then the bet was forged between Arun and Taredd to see who could catch a Human first.

Dain's bet had been on Taredd. Not because he thought Arun incapable of catching a Human, but because Demons were a lot better at tracking than Fae. At least, from what he'd seen, and he'd seen a lot.

They were an odd group of friends. Arun a Fae, Taredd

a Demon, and Dain a Shapeshifter, but it worked... they worked. If it hadn't been for Taredd and Arun, Dain wouldn't be alive.

He pissed off the wrong person when he was younger, and nearly paid the ultimate price. Thankfully, Taredd had stepped in with Arun, saving his life. Since then, the three of them had been inseparable.

Working as a team, they'd fought alongside each other during the war. Refusing to take sides with their own kind when the war broke out, they'd made their fair share of enemies, but none were powerful enough to take them on when they worked as a team.

It had always been just the three of them, but even that was about to change. No longer were they going to be three males working alongside each other to rid the world of Humans. Instead, they were going to be working together to keep them alive. At least, some of them.

Taredd had won the bet in more ways than one. He'd not only found and captured a Human female, but he'd taken her as his mate. Which was why everything was about to change, and why it was imperative that they found Arun.

Taredd wanted to take his new mate, Natalia, back to his home in the Demon realm, which was easier said than done. Admittedly, there was no safer place for her than Taredd's home, but it was going to be hell getting her there safely.

If they stood any chance, they were going to need Arun's help. But first, they needed to find him.

Not to mention Natalia refused to go anywhere until they found her friends. Unfortunately, they didn't have a clue where to look for them either.

The last time Natalia had seen them, they were heading through the mountain pass. She was supposed to meet them when she arrived, but before she could look for them, Taredd caught her.

So, she didn't have a clue where they were. All she could tell them was that they would be hiding out underground somewhere.

Yeah, they were definitely going to have their work cut out for them.

He was still reeling from the news of Taredd taking a Human as his mate. Out of the three of them, Taredd was the least likely to take a Human to his bed, let alone mate with one. He was trying to make sense of it all over a glass of whiskey or twenty.

If Dain had to guess, he'd say there were less than a handful of Humans left alive. He hoped he was wrong, but he doubted it. Trust Taredd to take one as his mate, making all their lives more complicated.

No matter how much he thought about it, or how much he drank, he still couldn't make sense of it.

He downed the last of the whiskey and pushed his glass away as he stood.

"Thanks," he said to the bartender.

He didn't hang around to see if the bartender said anything. He headed straight upstairs to the room he'd rented for the night. Tomorrow was going to be a long assed day, searching for Arun along with the female's friends.

Natalia, he reminded himself. *Her name is Natalia.*

From the sounds of it, she had a list of friends they needed to look for. He just hoped they weren't too late to find them alive, but only time would tell.

Chapter 3

"Who's on dinner duty tonight?" Amberly asked.

"I'll do it," Donovan volunteered.

"Thank you," she said.

The day after they arrived at the bunker, a couple of them went out in search of food supplies. Thankfully, they found enough to last them a few days, but at some point, they would need to look for more.

The main thing they were short on was firewood. It had been so cold, especially at night, that they had burned through what they had collected the first night. So, somebody would need to go out for more.

Since Donovan was cooking, that ruled him out. She debated asking the other men in the group to go out, but quickly changed her mind.

She hadn't left the bunker since they arrived, and

it was getting to her. She hadn't even snuck out after everyone had fallen asleep like she normally would.

So, she decided against asking the men to do the chore. They would only moan about it anyway.

She slipped on her shoes and pulled on her coat, zipping it up all the way before pulling the hood over her head.

"I'll collect some wood," she said as she headed towards the ladder. "I'll be back soon."

"Okay," Donovan said. "But take someone with you. It's getting dark outside."

"I'll come with you," Ellen said when Amberly turned back around.

"Thank you, Ellen," she said. "It shouldn't take us long."

"That's okay, it's not as if I've got anything else to do tonight," Ellen said.

"True," Amberly agreed. "None of us do."

"Yeah, I know," Ellen said, sighing. "Boring isn't it."

"Just a little, but it's better than being out there on the run," Amberly told her.

"Only just," Ellen said.

Amberly had to agree. It was even more boring than it usually was. At least when Natalia was there, she had some company. She couldn't really talk to the others like she could Natalia. Even Donovan was hit and miss some days.

She hoped Natalia was safe and well. Amberly didn't care if she found Bella or not, as long as she came back in one piece.

"Come on then, let's get this over and done with," Amberly said, heading up the ladder.

At the top of the ladder, she opened the hatch just enough for her to see outside. An icy blast hit her in the face, sending shivers racing down her spine.

When she was certain the coast was clear, she opened it all the way and climbed the rest of the way out. Ellen was hot on her heels.

It amazed Amberly how much colder it was. When they travelled to the other side of the mountain, none of them had imagined the temperature would be drastically different from what they were used to. But they were there now, they had to make the most of it.

As soon as they were outside, they didn't waste any time in collecting firewood. They picked up as many twigs and broken branches as they could find, dropping armfuls down into the bunker.

By the time they had collected enough firewood to last them a couple of days, it was completely dark outside.

Amberly's nerves were on edge as they made their way back to the bunker for the last time. The hairs on the back of her neck stood up, and she suddenly had a feeling they were being watched.

"Hurry," she whispered.

Ellen didn't ask what was wrong. She dropped the armful of twigs she had collected and instantly broke into a sprint as they raced back to the bunker.

As soon as they reached it, Ellen swung herself over the edge and climbed down the ladder first. Just as Amberly was about to follow, she was grabbed from behind and viciously thrown away from the bunker.

Pain radiated out from where she made impact with a large tree, knocking the wind out of her. She landed on the floor with a thud.

Stars threatened to take over her vision as she fought for air.

Before she had a chance to catch her breath, she heard screaming coming from the bunker.

It took her a moment to realise the monster had thrown her out the way so he could get inside the bunker before they could lock the door.

Shit!

Amberly tried scrambling to her feet, but her arms and legs refused to cooperate. One way or another, she needed to get inside the bunker and help the others.

Refusing to give up, Amberly got on her hands and knees and began crawling towards the bunker.

"Where do you think you're going?" a sinister voice said from above her.

Her head snapped up, and she came face to face with a monster. He would have appeared Human if it hadn't been for the glowing red rim around his eyes and the flash of fang as he grinned at her.

Great! The blood suckers are here.

Her mother had warned her about their kind. She called them Vampires. Whether that was what they actually were, she didn't know. She really hoped not though, because her mother told her they drained all the blood from their victims before discarding the lifeless bodies in a heap.

"Well? Where are you going?" he asked again.

Amberly's hand brushed against a large rock as he pulled her up to her feet. Acting on instinct, she picked it up. When she was within reaching distance of his face, she quickly swung her arm and smashed the rock into the side of his head.

"Fuck!" he shouted.

His hands shot to his face as he took a step backward, dropping her at the same time.

She landed on her knees with a thud. Pain shot up her thighs and reverberated through her body. She bit her tongue to stop from screaming.

Amberly didn't wait for the pain to subside. She jumped to her feet as fast as she could, and took off running for the bunker.

She swung her legs over the edge of the bunker and grabbed hold of the ladder. Hooking her feet on the outside of the ladder, she loosened her grip and let gravity take over her descent.

Her legs nearly gave out under her as she hit the bottom, but she managed to catch herself at the last second.

Screaming greeted her as she raced into the main living area, along with the sound of fighting. There was no way Donovan would give up without a fight, and she was right.

Fear clawed at her as she spotted him in the middle of the room. He was brandishing a thick branch in front of him as he tried in vain to keep the Vampires back.

"Run Amberly!" he shouted when he caught sight of her entering the room.

But it was too late. The Vampire she'd hit with the rock had joined them in the bunker.

"Got you," he snapped as he wrapped his arms around her waist, pinning her arms to her sides in the process. "Feisty little thing, aren't you?"

Amberly would not make it easy for him. She wasn't going without a fight either.

She tried in vain to wriggling out of his grip. When that didn't work, she threw her head backward and stomped on his foot. But that didn't faze him either. He held on to her with an iron grip.

She regretted dropping the rock after she hit him, it might have come in handy a second time.

"Get off me!" she screamed.

"I don't think so," he said, tightening his hold on her. "You're not getting away from me again."

"Get off her!" Donovan shouted.

He ran towards them, still swinging the branch in front of him.

One of the Vampires blocking his way stepped to the side, letting him go past. As soon as he did, the Vampire spun around and grabbed the back of his shirt.

Donovan's feet left the ground as he was yanked backward. A moment later he hit the hard floor with a loud thud. Flat on his back, pain contorted his face as he looked up at the ceiling. She could see the wind had been knocked out of him, just as it had her when she hit the tree.

Before he could recover, the Vampire leaned down and snatched the branch out of his hands.

"I'll have that," he said smugly.

"Fuck you!" Donovan tried snatching it back, but the Vampire was faster.

"Get rid of this," he said, throwing it to someone behind Amberly before turning his attention back on Donovan. "Get up."

Not giving Donovan the chance to move, he bent back down and grabbed him by the shirt before pulling him to his feet.

With Donovan now unarmed and out of the way, more Vampires' filed into the bunker, subduing everyone else within seconds.

"See? I told you they would be here," a familiar voice said from behind Amberly.

"What have you done Bella?" Ellen demanded.

"Bella?" Amberly asked in disbelief.

"Yes, Amberly, it's me," Bella said smugly.

She strolled into the room as if she didn't have a care in the world. Smiling as she looked around at everyone being held back by the Vampires.

Bella stopped in front of her. "I bet you didn't think you'd see me again, did you?"

Amberly didn't know what the hell had happened to her, but she wasn't the same person anymore. Not if she was happy to hand over her own kind to the monsters. The Bella she knew wouldn't do that to her friends.

After everything they'd all been through together, how could she just hand them all over to the monsters? And not just any monsters. Vampires.

Out of all the species to hand them over to, Vampires

were the worst.

"What have you done?" Amberly asked.

Fear for Natalia clawed at Amberly, but as much as she wanted to ask Bella about her, she didn't dare mention her in front of the Vampires. If they didn't know about her already, then she didn't want to be the one to tip them off that she was out there all alone.

"I did what I needed to," she said. "What any of you would have done if you were in my situation."

She spun around as she spoke, looking at each of them in turn.

"None of us would sell out our own kind just to save our own skin," Donovan spat. "You're no Human. You're a monster, just like the rest of them."

"Tell yourself whatever you want," she said, lifting her chin as she looked at him. "I know you would do the same."

"No, I wouldn't," he snarled. "Because I am nothing like you."

"Keep telling yourself that," Bella laughed. "You, for one, are more like me than you think."

"You're scum," he spat.

"See," she said, ignoring Donovan's comment as she turned back towards Amberly. "I told you they'd be here."

Even though she was looking at Amberly, she spoke to the Vampire holding her.

"Yes, you were right," the Vampire said.

"So, I'm free to go now?" Bella asked eagerly.

Amberly stared at Bella. She couldn't really be stupid

enough to believe the Vampires would just let her go because she'd handed over the rest of them, could she? Had she gone completely insane in the short time they'd been apart?

She must have if she thought they were going to just let her go on her merry old way.

"Soon," the Vampire told her.

"But…"

"No but's," he said. "You'll be free to go when we've finished with you and not a moment sooner."

Amberly could tell Bella wasn't happy with the news, but she didn't argue about it. Instead, she stood silently with her arms crossed in front of her chest. She looked like a toddler that hadn't got its own way.

What Bella didn't seem to grasp, was how much danger she was in. Even Amberly knew they weren't going to let her go. They never let anyone go. Even children weren't exempt from them.

If a child was caught by any other species, they would be sold to the highest bidder and either kept as a slave, or used as food. With Vampires, there was no selling involved. It didn't matter if they caught a child or an adult; they fed upon their prisoners.

Amberly had known a few people who'd lost their child. It didn't matter whether they were caught by Vampires or another species, they were never seen or heard from again.

Her heart broke for the parents and the children. She couldn't imagine losing a child like that, but she knew all too well what it was like to lose a parent. She still grieved the loss of her mother, even though many years had passed.

She never had the chance to meet her father because he died before she was born, but her mother used to talk about him often.

"What are we going to do with all of you?" the Vampire holding her asked.

There was no doubt in her mind he was the one in charge. It was just her luck to piss off the one in charge of all the rest.

Maybe it wasn't so wise to hit him with a rock after all, she thought.

Unfortunately, she couldn't turn back the clocks. She would have to live with the consequences of her actions, however short that might be.

Chapter 4

After spending the night under the stars, Dain wasn't looking forward to riding in the back of the cart all day. He would much rather walk than be pulled along by a horse as he sat in a rickety old cart.

Unfortunately, they didn't know how long it would take them to find Natalia's friends or Arun. It could be days before they came across either of their tracks, which wasn't a problem for him or Taredd, but Natalia wouldn't be able to last that long on foot.

Humans weren't able to travel as far and fast as him and Taredd. They would need to stop regularly so Natalia could rest, but they didn't have the time. So, they needed the horse and cart.

Dain had to admit, it came in handy. He'd hardly slept because he'd kept watch for most of the night, so he took the opportunity to catch some z's while he could.

It wasn't long after he dozed off that Natalia suddenly woke him shouting 'stop'.

She'd spotted one of the Human hide-outs from a distance. Thankfully, she told them what she'd spotted instead of just running off into the woods.

Before she made it to the open hatch, Taredd stopped her and sent Dain off ahead to check it out. The last thing they needed was to walk into a trap.

So, Taredd stayed outside with Natalia while Dain descended into an underground hide-out.

He could smell the coppery scent of blood before he even stepped foot inside, so he knew instantly that something had happened, he just didn't know what. The further down he went, the stronger the scent grew.

As he stepped through the entrance to what he assumed was the main living area, the first thing he noticed was a massive puddle of blood in the middle of the room. There were signs of a struggle everywhere he looked, but the blood was a stark contrast to the grey concrete.

He couldn't tell how many people had been involved, or who the blood belonged to, but he picked up multiple scents mingled in with that of the blood. Some were stronger than others, meaning they were more recent, but that still didn't tell Dain much about what happened.

It soon became clear on his search of the rest of the bunker, that the destruction hadn't only been confined to the other room. The entire place had been turned upside down.

It looked like someone had been searching for something, which made absolutely no sense at all. It wasn't as if Humans had many possessions nowadays, but they definitely owned nothing of value. At least, nothing the other species would consider valuable.

Natalia had broken down in tears when she saw the state of the place. Fearing the worst had happened to her friends.

Dain didn't want to be the one to tell her she was right to fear the worst, because the worst had more than likely happened. Since all of her friends were adults, even young adults, the likelihood of them still being alive was extremely slim.

It would only be slightly different if they were children. But even that depended on who found them.

Not all species were the same. Some weren't interested in keeping the Humans alive, and would kill on sight. Some kept them alive for a short time, either as a food source, or to torture.

Very few, however, kept them alive for a long time. Usually, it was only the children that were kept as slaves, but occasionally, one of them might take a liking to an adult Human and keep them as a slave.

On those occasions, it wasn't to the benefit of the Human. No, they wished for death rather than have to deal with their duties, which generally consisted of pleasuring their master.

Both he and Taredd had assured her Arun hadn't been the one responsible for the carnage in his bid to win the bet. They hadn't lied when they told her Arun would need to capture a Human alive, or risk being seen as cheating. But that wasn't the only reason they doubted it was him.

Arun was a lot like Dain in the way he felt about the Humans, more so than Taredd. He didn't enjoy killing Humans, but he saw it as a necessary evil, just as Dain did. It was either a quick and clean kill from him, or a long drawn out one by somebody else.

"We need to find her friends," Taredd said.

Dain looked over to see Natalia's sleeping form on the back of the cart.

They hadn't stayed at the bunker for too long, just in case the people who attacked her friends returned. The last thing they needed was to be caught unawares and backed into a corner. Dain fought better when he had plenty of space to shape shift.

At least they knew they were on the right track looking for her friends. She confirmed it was them that were staying there by the items lying around the place.

She collected a few of the items before they got on their way again. Gently placing each item neatly in a bag as tears streamed down her face.

Dain couldn't help but feel for her. He knew what it was like to lose someone you loved. It tore your heart to shreds, but more so when they are taken from you so violently.

He still had scars on his heart, and would forever carry them with him as a reminder of what he had and lost.

Natalia barely spoke a word for the rest of the day. She picked at her dinner before pushing it away, saying she was too tired to eat. Neither Dain nor Taredd stopped her from climbing in the back of the cart.

It took a while, but eventually her soft weeping stopped as she fell asleep. There was nothing she could do to help her friends, so it was best she slept to pass the time instead.

"I know," Dain said. "But it's not going to be easy. That's if they're even still alive."

"Yeah, I know," he said. "But I've promised her we'll try. I can't let her down."

"Well, I wouldn't want to be in your shoes if it turns out they're all dead," Dain said.

"I hope it doesn't come to that."

"The likelihood of one or two of them still being alive is very slim, let alone all of them," Dain pointed out. "I hope you've prepared her for that."

"Kind of," he said. "I didn't want to upset her more than she already is."

Taredd was digging himself into a hole. He was better off being honest with Natalia. The sooner she came to terms with the possibility of not seeing her friends again, the sooner she could get past the mourning stage.

"What about Arun?" Dain asked. "We could really do with his help."

"I know," Taredd agreed. "But unless we can find him along the way, he'll have to wait. I'm not holding of rescuing her friends. The longer we leave it, the more likely it is we'll be too late. As it is, we don't know how long they've been missing."

If they weren't already too late. He may not have said the words, but Dain knew Taredd had been thinking it.

"I'm not saying to hold off," he said. "But we don't know what happened, or who is involved. We could end up being outnumbered."

"We've been outnumbered before," Taredd reminded him.

More than once, but that wasn't the point he was trying to get at.

"Yes, but usually there's the three of us," Dain pointed out.

"We did okay getting Natalia back without Arun's help," Taredd said.

Yes, they had, but she'd only been held captive by half a dozen lesser Demons. So, yeah, they'd got her back easily enough, but that didn't mean it was going to be the same for her friends.

"We don't know what the situation is with her friends though," Dain said. "It could be a hell of a lot worse. We could be walking into something we can't get ourselves out of."

"I know," Taredd said. "But we need to try."

Taredd was out of his mind, but Dain was just stupid enough that he was going to help him.

"Fine," Dain said. "What do you want me to do?"

"Great," Taredd said. "I need you to shift into an animal."

"Again?" Dain asked.

Last time Taredd asked him to shift, he had to turn into a mouse and crawl around a dingy building that was occupied by lesser Demons. It was disgusting, to say the least.

"Yeah, sorry," Taredd said, looking anything but sorry. "On the upside, at least it's not a mouse this time, and you're not crawling around a building either."

Dain already knew what the answer would be, but he still asked the question, anyway. "What animal is it this time?"

"A dog," Taredd said. "It can be any type of canine you want, but they've got the best sense of smell."

"Oh, wow, I get to choose," he said sarcastically. "And actually, bears have a much better sense of smell than a dog. They can pick up a scent from miles away."

"Okay, a bear then," Taredd said.

Dain shook his head. After all the years they'd been hunting together, Taredd still didn't have a clue about animals. It was sad, really. Dain knew a hell of a lot about Demons and Fae from hanging around with Taredd and Arun.

"I really do appreciate your help," Natalia said, sitting up in the back of the cart.

Dain hadn't even realised she was awake, and by the look on Taredd's face, he hadn't either.

He could see the plea for help in her eyes, and he couldn't bring himself to say no to her. He may end up regretting the decision, but he would cross that bridge when the time came.

"It's okay," he said. "I don't mind."

Natalia gave him a small smile. "Thank you."

She must have been crying the entire time she'd been curled up in the cart instead of sleeping. The tears on her eyelashes glistened in the light from the fire, and her eyes still had unshed tears in them.

"It's no problem," he assured her.

"Get to it then," Taredd said, nudging him.

Dain growled at Taredd before shifting into a bear. The large animal soon filled up the space around the campfire.

He was careful not to singe his fur on the flickering flames.

Natalia picked up an item of clothing she'd packed into the bag at the bunker and held it out to him.

"This belongs to Amberly," she said. "If we can find her, we should be able to find the rest of them."

As soon as he had the scent, he nodded his head, and she tucked the item back in the bag after folding it neatly again.

"You lead the way, and we'll follow behind in the cart," Taredd said.

Dain nodded. He didn't need to sniff around the area looking for clues. As soon as Natalia held out the item of clothing belonging to her friend, he'd picked up the scent trail.

Instead of waiting for them to pack everything up, he began following the scent. They could easily spot his black coat from a distance, so he wasn't concerned about them losing sight of him.

If he was trying to hide from them, then it would be a completely different matter. Since he needed them to follow, he made sure they could see him.

It soon became clear they were on the same path her friends had taken all along. The scent was getting stronger and stronger by the minute, meaning they were quickly catching up.

If they hadn't stopped when they did, there was a high possibility they could have caught up with her friends already. He wasn't about to tell Natalia that thought. He didn't want her getting any more upset than she already was.

Chapter 5

No matter how much she struggled, she couldn't break free from the bonds that held her down. Her mind raced with a thousand thoughts as her heart broke into a million pieces.

She was the last person alive in the group. Everyone else had died at the hands of the Vampires.

The stories her mother told her as a girl of the Vampires, weren't nearly as bad as what they were like in real life. Amberly quickly realised her mother had sugar-coated a lot of her stories.

She couldn't blame her mother. She would do exactly the same thing if she ever had children. But that wasn't likely to happen now.

No, at the rate she was going, she would join her friends in the afterlife very soon. That's if there even was an afterlife. For all she knew, it could just be another story her mother made up.

She couldn't shake the image of Donovan's face as the Vampires fed upon him. His eyes had pleaded with her to help, as his face twisted with agony. But there was nothing she could do, nothing she could say, that would stop them from their task.

Donovan didn't give in to them like the others did. He fought to break free as they slowly drained the life from him.

She was made to watch as one by one her friends were drained of blood. Their lifeless bodies were dropped like rag-dolls on the floor in front of her.

She wished that was the worst she'd seen, but it wasn't. What they did to Bella was far worse than anything they put her friends through.

As much as she tried to feel sorry for the woman, she couldn't. If Bella hadn't walked away from the group, none of it would have happened and her friends would still be alive.

She still couldn't believe Bella had done it. She couldn't understand how Bella could hate her own kind so much that she'd turn them over to the monsters.

No matter how much Amberly disliked someone, she would never even consider turning them over to the monsters.

Bella was incredibly naïve to think the Vampires would let her go free when she handed them over. She didn't know what they said to her that made her think otherwise, but whatever it was, Amberly wouldn't have believed a single word they said.

She wouldn't believe their promises of freedom, and she certainly wouldn't just hand over possibly the last of her kind. She'd rather die than betray her friends, her family.

Because that's what they were, family. They bickered, they argued, but most of all, they looked out for each other. Had each other's backs. At least, that's how it was supposed to be.

She prayed Natalia hadn't caught up with Bella. She would hate to think of her friend... her sister... going through what she'd seen the other women in her group go through. Or what she'd gone through herself.

She hadn't dared mention Natalia in front of the Vampires, and thankfully, Bella hadn't mentioned her either. Amberly didn't know if that was a good thing or not, but she was taking it as a good sign that Natalia didn't catch up with her.

If she had, Amberly was sure Bella would have rubbed it in that she'd already handed over Natalia. Since she hadn't, Amberly was hoping for the best.

Unfortunately, she hadn't been exempt from some of the deprived things the other women and Bella had been made to suffer. She was still suffering long after her friends had taken their final breath.

She didn't know why the Vampires were keeping her alive when they had killed everyone else, but she didn't think it was for a good reason. Not knowing from one minute to the next if they were finally going to end her the same way as her friends, had her constantly on edge every time they came in the tent.

Was it some kind of sick game they liked to play? Had they done the same with other Humans? Or was it just her?

Did they get a buzz from making her constantly worry if the next time they entered the tent that it might be the last time? Or did they have something else, something worse, planned for her?

Was that why they were keeping her alive? Because they had something worse in store for her? She really hoped not.

Amberly refused to beg them to kill her, but she didn't know how much more she could take before she finally broke.

Having her body used against her will was slowly taking its toll. Not only physically, but mentally as well.

Every time they did things to her body that she didn't want them to do, she would disappear into the deep recesses of her mind. A place where they couldn't reach her... where they couldn't hurt her.

She pictured herself as a cat, curled up in a box while waiting for the storm to pass. But Amberly didn't know how much longer it would work. She could already feel herself slipping back to reality before she was ready, before they left her alone.

She would spend the entire time there if she could. Unfortunately, she was only able to take herself there while the Vampires were doing despicable things to her body. The rest of the time she had to deal with being tied up in a tent.

Being tied up wouldn't be as bad if they'd at least let her wear some clothes, or even cover herself with a blanket, but that wasn't to be. They ripped her clothes from her body as soon as they arrived at their campsite, and she hadn't been allowed to cover up since.

Amberly wasn't sure how long ago that was. She could've been there for a matter of hours, or she could've been there for days.

Time seemed to pass differently when she was curled up as a cat inside her mind, but she didn't care. It was a hell of a lot better than watching helplessly as they abused her body.

A shiver raced down her spine, freezing the blood in her veins, as one of the Vampires entered the tent. He walked toward her with an evil grin on his face, flashing his fangs at the same time.

She could tell by the look on his face that she would not like what was coming next. Dread filled her at the thought of him touching her.

Amberly wouldn't beg for death, but that didn't stop her from praying for it.

Chapter 6

Shortly after they set off, Dain stopped and turned back. They were getting close.

He'd been right. Her friends were a lot closer than they originally thought. In fact, it had taken them less than half a day to get there. There was only a short distance left between them, but Dain didn't dare get any closer.

Natalia's friends weren't alone, and he knew exactly who they were with. Vampires.

He'd picked up the scent as soon as he'd shifted, but he hadn't said anything. He hoped the scents had just crossed paths at some point, which was why he hadn't said anything.

But now he knew for definite. Vampires raided the bunker and had taken Natalia's friends with them.

The chances of her friends still being alive were

growing slimmer by the second. If they didn't act now, it would be too late.

Since the risk of being seen was high, he'd purposely kept his distance and stayed downwind. Vampires didn't have the best sense of smell, but it was good enough to pick up their scent if they ventured too close.

They did, however, have incredible hearing and eyesight. So, it would not be easy sneaking around their campsite to look for survivors.

When Taredd noticed he was heading back to them, he pulled the horse to a stop and waited.

"What's wrong?" Taredd asked when Dain reached them.

Not wasting any time, he quickly shifted back to Human form so he could talk to them.

"We're getting close," he said.

"Really?" Taredd asked. "But we haven't gone far."

"I know," he said. "But trust me, they're just up ahead."

"What are we waiting for then?" Natalia asked. "If they're just ahead of us, then we need to get going."

"No," Taredd said. "Dain was right to stop. We need to know what we're walking into. We don't want to cause more problems for ourselves by going in half-cocked. Plus, it puts your friends' lives more at risk if we go storming in there. So, we need to know what's waiting for us."

"Which means we need to scout the area," Dain told her.

"Okay," she said.

He could tell she wasn't happy about it, but she didn't argue.

As much as she wanted to rescue her friends, they wouldn't be any help if they were caught themselves. Or worse, killed. So, they needed to be prepared.

"You should be far enough away that they won't be able to pick up your scent, or catch sight of you," he said. "So, wait here while I check it out."

"Did you pick up anything?" Taredd asked.

Dain knew what he meant. Had he picked up the scents of who they were up against as he tracked down her friends, and the answer was yes.

"I did," he said.

"And?" Taredd asked.

"Let me check it out first," Dain said. "To make sure I'm right."

"Okay," Taredd said. "Make sure you stay out of sight."

"I will do," Dain said before shifting again.

Since bears might not be native to the area, he shifted into a raven instead. There were always plenty of them flying above Vampire camps, no matter where in the world they were.

They were drawn to them because of all the dead bodies the Vampires left lying around, so he should have no problem blending in.

Within minutes, he was circling above the Vampire campsite. And as he suspected, there were plenty of ravens doing the same thing.

So used to seeing them, the Vampires didn't even look

up as they milled about camp.

Shit! This is exactly what I was dreading.

He couldn't see all the Vampires, but with the number of tents in the area, he didn't doubt there would be more than just a few. They weren't dealing with a handful; they were dealing with a horde.

With any other species, there could still be a chance her friends were alive. But with a horde of Vampires, the chances were slim to none.

Vampires were notorious for taking no prisoners. And if they did, the prisoners never lasted long. They drained their victims dry, and then discarded the body as if it was nothing more than rubbish.

Dain didn't hold out much hope Natalia's friends were still alive. He wasn't looking forward to breaking the bad news to her.

Before turning around and heading back to Taredd and Natalia, he took a closer look inside the camp. Swooping down low, he flew between the tents. Peeking inside any that were left open as he passed by.

He noticed something in one tent, so he circled round for a better look. Landing on the floor by the entrance, he crept over to peek inside.

Shit! He swore.

A female was tied to a makeshift bed inside the tent, but that wasn't what worried him most. No, it was the Vampire in there with her that worried him. There was no telling if she'd still be alive when he comes back with Taredd, but he couldn't risk trying to break her out on his own.

If she was able to walk out of there on her own two feet it would be a different matter, but he had a feeling she wouldn't be able to stand, let alone make it out of the campsite without being seen.

Unfortunately, he couldn't tell if it was Natalia's friend or not. Either way, they couldn't leave the female in the hands of the Vampires. He was amazed she was still alive, especially if it was one of Natalia's friends.

There wasn't much he could do on his own, and definitely not while there was so much activity going on in the campsite. So, he took to the sky again and headed back to Taredd and Natalia.

Now he knew what they were up against, they could plan what to do next. He just hoped for Natalia's sake that it was one of her friends and that they're still alive when he returns.

He flew back to Taredd and Natalia as fast as he could. Thankfully, they'd moved a little further away from the Vampires, but he was still able to find them easily.

They had set up camp while he'd been gone, and now sat around a fire when he returned.

Shifting in mid-flight a short distance away, he landed gracefully on his feet. His long strides covered the remaining distance.

"We have a problem," Dain said as soon as he reached them.

"What?" Taredd asked.

"Vampires. And lots of them."

"Shit!" Taredd said, running a hand through his hair.

"What's wrong?" Natalia asked.

"Vampires took your friends," Dain told her.

"I don't understand," she said.

He could see the confusion on her face. It was obvious she hadn't crossed paths with Vampires before, otherwise she'd know how bad a situation it was.

"Vampires aren't known for keeping anyone alive," Dain explained. "If it were any other species, there might have been a chance your friends could still be alive. Unfortunately, the chance of your friends surviving in a Vampire camp, is very slim. So, there's a very high possibility your friends are already dead."

He hadn't mentioned the female in the tent yet because he didn't want her to get her hopes up.

"No," she said adamantly. "I know they're still alive. I don't know how, but I know it."

"Natalia," Taredd said sympathetically.

"No," she said. "It doesn't matter what you say, I know they're still alive, and I'm not going anywhere until I find them. You don't have to help me, but I'm not stopping until I find them. Vampires or not, I don't care who has my friends."

Dain hoped she was right, but the chances of that being the case were getting slimmer by the minute.

"I promised to help you," Taredd said to her. "And I keep my promises."

"Thank you," she said as tears gathered in her eyes.

"Tell me what you know," Taredd said, turning to Dain.

Dain filled them in on what he'd found. The campsite, the Vampires, and the Human he'd spotted.

He tried to make it clear to Natalia that he couldn't be certain if the Human was one of her friends or not. But that didn't seem to matter to her. She was adamant it was one of her friends.

If he'd shifted into another animal with a better sense of smell, he might have been able to tell if it was her friend Amberly. But the risk had been too high at that point.

Being seen by the Vampires wouldn't have been the best idea, especially since they were planning to sneak back in to rescue the female.

"There's got to be more," Natalia finally said.

"More what?" he asked, confused.

"There's got to be more people," she said. "There can't only be one person left."

Tears streaked silently down her cheeks as she spoke. Dain wished he had better news for her, but he wouldn't lie to her.

It would be a miracle if any of her friends were still alive. For all he knew, the female he'd seen could have absolutely nothing to do with Natalia.

"I'm sorry," he said. "I only saw one person."

"But that doesn't mean there isn't more," she said.

"If Dain only saw one person, it's likely the rest are already dead," Taredd said. "I'm sorry, Natalia, but they don't normally keep prisoners alive, let alone in separate places."

Taredd was right. If there had been more, they should be in the same place as the female he saw.

Once they rescued the female, they'd know if there

were any other survivors. Until then, it was anyone's guess. And if it did turn out to be one of her friends, hopefully they'd be able to tell them what happened to the others.

"Can we at least look for other survivors while we're there?" she asked. When neither of them answered straight away, she added. "We are still going there, aren't we? To rescue the person Dain saw?"

"Well, we are," Taredd said, indicating himself and Dain. "But you're not. It's way too dangerous for you to go into a Vampire camp."

Dain was staying well and truly out of this one. As much as he agreed with Taredd that it was too dangerous, he certainly would not tell Natalia she couldn't go.

If Human females were anything like Shapeshifter females, then there was no way he was getting involved. Shapeshifter females didn't take kindly to being told what they could and couldn't do, and would have the balls of anyone who tried to tell them.

"Okay," Natalia said, surprising them both.

Taredd was the first to recover from the shook of how easily that had been. Closing his mouth from where it had dropped open, Taredd smiled softly at her.

It was clear to see how much he cared for her after such a short time together. Only an idiot wouldn't be able to see it.

"I promise, we'll look for others," he swore.

"I know you will," she said. "I trust you."

Well, that's a first.

Never in his life had Dain heard a Human say they

trusted a Demon before. It was strange, but nice to hear. And it was just more proof that things were changing. Proof that Humans could coexist with other species.

Now, they just needed to show everyone else, which was a hell of a lot easier said than done.

He just hoped she hadn't agreed to stay behind so easily, only to ignore them later and follow, anyway. He could understand her wanting to help get her friends back, but she couldn't do it at the risk of herself or others.

If she went with them, she would probably end up getting in the way instead of helping them. Or worse, getting herself caught. Especially if she decided to go it alone.

The last thing they needed was for Natalia to get herself caught. They already had the female to rescue, and her friends to search for. They didn't need to add her to the mix as well.

Taredd wrapped his arms protectively around Natalia, and she smiled up at him.

"That's good to know," he said, kissing her forehead. "I promise never to break your trust."

"I know you won't," she said.

They spent the next half hour hashing out a plan of action. There was no point waiting until night fell again. With Vampires, it didn't make a blind bit of difference what time of the day or night they went in. Plus, it would be dark before long anyway.

Unlike the one's Humans wrote about, Vampires could walk around in broad daylight without bursting into flames. Garlic did fuck all, but a stake in the heart would kill them, but it would kill any species.

Dain must admit, he preferred to just rip the heads off. It was much easier and quicker than trying to stab the fuckers through the heart.

Dain could see it turning into a bloodbath if they weren't careful. He just hoped the female was still alive by the time they got there, and that she was one of Natalia's friends. Otherwise, they would be risking a hell of a lot for nothing.

"We'll be back as soon as we can," Taredd said when they were ready. "Stay here, and stay hidden."

"I will," she told him.

He could see Taredd didn't want to leave her on her own, but Dain couldn't break the female out on his own, so he had no choice. They certainly couldn't take her with them. It would be more dangerous than leaving her behind.

"Go," she said. "I'll be fine."

With one last look, Taredd follow Dain into the woods.

It didn't take them long to make their way to the Vampires camp. Thankfully, they didn't see anyone wondering around the woods outside of the camp on their way there. Hopefully, they would have the same luck on the way out again.

Darkness had descended by the time they reached the outer tents. Giving them added cover as they sneak around the campsite.

"That's a few more Vampires than you gave the impression there were," Taredd spoke as quietly as he could.

It was barely above a whisper, so he wasn't heard by the Vampires, but Dain could hear him loud and clear.

"It shouldn't be a problem," Dain said just as quietly. "As long as we don't get caught."

"Yeah," Taredd said sarcastically. "It's never a problem if we don't get caught."

Even in the darkness, Dain could see Taredd rolling his eyes.

"What?" he asked. "It's a good plan."

"Shut the fuck up and let's get this over with," Taredd said.

Well, there's no time like the present.

Neither of them spoke a word as they crept among the tents, sticking to the shadows as best they could. Taredd followed closely behind Dain as he made his way back to the tent he'd seen the female in earlier.

"They were in here," he whispered when they were outside the correct one.

"Okay," Taredd said. "We need to see what's going on in there."

"I know. Wait here and I'll take a look," Dain said.

"Be quick," Taredd told him. "I have a feeling we don't have long."

Dain had the same feeling.

Shifting into a mouse, he quickly scurried under the side of the tent. It took a second for his eyes to adjust to the bright light inside.

They were definitely in the right tent. By the looks of it, they were just in time as well. But that wasn't what had him rushing outside to get Taredd.

No, that was all to do with the female inside. It turned out Natalia was right all along. At least one of her friends was still alive. Unfortunately, she was the one chained to the floor inside the tent.

As soon as he slipped under the canvas, her scent hit him like a ton of bricks. It was mingled with sweat, blood, and other things he'd rather not think about.

"We're definitely in the right place," Dain said, not bothering to keep his voice as low as before.

In fact, he hoped the sound of his voice right outside the tent would make the Vampires pause, at least long enough for them to get in there.

"What did you see?" Taredd asked.

"The good news is, it looks like the same Human as earlier," he said. "The bad news is, it's definitely Natalia's friend, and she isn't alone. There's two Vamps in there with her."

"Shit!" Taredd said.

"That's not all," Dain shook his head at what he'd seen. "She's tied down spread eagle with nothing covering her. From what I could see, she's covered in cuts and bruises."

"Shit," Taredd said.

"You don't know the half of it," Dain said. "It wasn't a pretty sight. They have definitely been having fun with her."

Whether it was Natalia's friend or not, they couldn't leave a Human there. Especially a female Human. But thankfully, it was Natalia's friend. How much of her was left when the dust settled, they'd have to wait and see.

There was no doubt she would have a lot of healing to do, both physically and mentally. Hopefully, she was strong enough to pull through both.

Without another word, Dain and Taredd went in after her.

Chapter 7

After initially being taken to a large round tent where she was made to watch the Vampires feed upon her friends, Amberly was moved to a smaller tent where she was tied to a makeshift bed on the floor.

It wouldn't have been that bad if they'd left her clothing on, but they had torn her clothes from her body when she first arrived and hadn't bothered covering her since. The rough, unforgiving ropes were a constant reminder she was no longer free.

Her wrists and ankles were rubbed raw from where she had fought against the Vampires. She tried to untie the rope, but she only tightened it.

A small fire in the centre of the room was the only heat source she had. It wasn't too bad in the daytime, but at night, it barely kept her from shivering.

One after the other, the Vampires continually paid her visits. They never left her alone for long.

They would use her body as they fed from her, and there was absolutely nothing she could do to stop them. She couldn't fight them, and there was no point screaming because even if someone heard her, they were unlikely to come to her rescue.

Amberly lost track of how many times she'd been fed upon. Or how many times her body had been used. She didn't even know how long she'd been in their care.

After a while, her mind couldn't take it anymore and finally snapped, but not in the way she would have thought. She didn't know how she managed it, or how it was even possible, but she was able to escape into her mind.

Nothing could hurt her there, not even the Vampires. Curled up in the dark recesses of her mind, she felt no pain, no anger, and no sorrow. There was nothing but complete and utter silence.

It was like floating through a black hole in space. There was no light, just the steady beating of her heart to remind her she was still alive.

The first time she disappeared into her mind, she thought they had finally taken too much blood and killed her. It was only when she came back to reality that she realised she was still in the land of the living.

Her heart sank when she opened her eyes and looked around the dark, dank tent. The only thing that made her feel any better, was the fact she was alone again. The Vampire who'd been in there with her had finished what he was doing and left.

Each time one of them paid her a visit after that, she would disappear into her mind. Hiding out in the darkness until she was once again alone. Blissfully unaware of what her body was going through, she took refuge in memories of her friends and of her mother.

It was so peaceful, she never wanted to return to reality. Unfortunately, she couldn't make it last. All too soon her mind would snap back and she'd find herself tied up in the tent again.

The Vampire she'd hit with the rock had taken a special interest in her. He visited her regularly, and each visit was worse than the one before.

The first time he came to her, he was alone and only drank from her. But all too soon he began using her body like all rest, and not just on his own. On his last visit, he'd brought a friend with him.

Amberly shuddered as images flashed in her mind of what they had done to her. Even locked away in her mind, she wasn't able to completely escape. She knew what was happening, could see what they were doing to her. But instead of being in the moment and experiencing it first-hand, it was like watching it from a distance while trapped in a black box.

Most of the time she was able to look away and concentrate on the memories of her mother and friends. Other times she was unable to look away and was made to watch as they did despicable things to her body.

Out of all the Vampires that had paid her a visit, the one she'd hit with a rock was the worst of them.

Amberly's heart sank when he strolled into the tent with another one of his friends. She knew what was coming, and she didn't want any part of it, but there was nothing she could do.

Even if she broke free somehow, she still wouldn't make it very far. It was extremely cold during the day, but it was even worse come nightfall. The freezing temperatures at night could easily kill her.

If she stood any chance in making it on her own, she would need plenty of warm clothes and blankets. But she didn't have a stitch of clothing, let alone warm clothing.

When they had stripped her, they had destroyed her clothes. Ripping them to shreds until there was nothing left but tattered remains on the floor. Apart from the blankets she was lying on, there was absolutely nothing in the room she could use.

Not that she wanted to take the blankets with her. The pungent smell of sweat and blood constantly assaulted her nose, while the rough material scratched her raw wherever it touched her bare skin.

At that moment in time, Amberly would much rather face the freezing temperatures naked then deal with the two Vampires stood before her.

She fought back bile as they stared down at her with hunger in their eyes.

"What shall we do with you tonight?" the Vampire she had hit asked.

"Nothing," she breathed.

The word was barely louder than a whisper, yet they

both heard it.

"Now, where's the fun in that?" he chuckled.

"I've got an idea what we can do," his friend said, grinning as he rubbed his hands together. "But it involves one more person."

"Ooh, I like the way you think," he said.

"Good," his friend said. "Because he should be here any minute."

Amberly didn't like the idea of another Vampire joining them. One of them was bad enough. Two was a nightmare, but three? No, just kill her now and get it over with because she couldn't take anymore.

Just as they were about to strip, two newcomers entered the tent, but neither were the Vampire the other two had been talking about.

One of the newcomers could've passed for Human if it hadn't been for his glowing amber eyes. They stood out against his tanned skin and dark hair.

Fear like no other sliced through her at the sight of the Shapeshifter, followed swiftly by desire.

Her mother had always told her that Shapeshifter were the worst of all the monsters. She would tell her stories about how despicable they were, how evil. Not once had she mentioned how attractive they were.

She made them out to be gruesome creatures that took many guises, mostly as animals, and would rip her to shreds if they ever caught her. Amberly had many nightmares where monsters with glowing amber eyes would eat her alive, and now one of them stood before her.

She dragged her eyes off him to look at the other newcomer.

There was no way the Shapeshifters friend could pass for Human. His red skin was a dead giveaway that he was a Demon. Not to mention the two black horns protruding from the top of his head and curling backward.

Amberly had never heard of Shapeshifters and Demons mixing before. Past experience, and what she'd garnered from other Humans, the monsters generally stuck to their own kind. She knew they would mingle in towns and villages, but she never thought they would travel together.

From the looks of it, the two in front of her were doing more than just travelling together. She couldn't help but wonder what their story was.

"Excuse me, guys," the Shapeshifter spoke first. His deep voice sent shivers down her spine, and not the bad kind. "We're looking for a couple of bloodsuckers, can you help us out?"

"Who the fuck are you?" the Vampire she hit demanded.

"Doesn't really matter who we are," the Demon said. "What matters is what we're going to do to you."

"Oh, yeah," the other Vampire said. "And what's that?"

"Oh, nothing much," the Shapeshifter said as he shrugged one shoulder. "We're just going to kill you both and take the female."

Both Vampires burst out laughing at the newcomers.

A mixture of hope and dread swirled around inside

her. She wanted to get out of there, to get as far away from the Vampires as she could possibly get. But at the expense of trading one prison for another?

She wasn't sure her mind and body could cope with much more. She would be stupid to think the newcomers were rescuing her out of the goodness of their heart.

Even knowing she would probably be trading one prison for another, hope continued to grow inside her. Anything had to be better than what she had been dealing with.

The Shapeshifter and Demon shared a look as the Vampires continued to laugh. She could feel the tension building between them while they waited patiently for her captors to stop laughing.

"You do know where you are, don't you?" one Vampire asked after a couple of minutes.

"Of course we do," the Demon said.

"Then you know the likelihood of that happening, is very slim," the Vampire said.

"Would you like to place a bet?" the Shapeshifter asked with a raised eyebrow.

The Demon rolled his eyes as he turned to face his friend. "What is it with you and betting at the moment? Anyone would think you have a gambling problem."

"Nah, I don't have a gambling problem," the Shapeshifter said. "It's just a bit of fun to pass the time."

"Well, I'm not placing a bet with these guys," the Demon said. "They're not going to be around long enough to pay up."

"Yeah, true," he agreed.

It was like some fucked up dream. And by the looks of it, she wasn't the only one that thought so.

The two Vampires were like statues, their mouths wide open as they watched the newcomers talk among themselves as if they weren't in the middle of a Vampire camp. It would have been funny if she hadn't been chained to a makeshift bed on the floor completely naked.

Neither of the newcomers were paying attention to anybody else in the tent. They were so focused on their own discussion; they didn't notice the Vampires snap out of whatever trance they were in and creep forward.

She knew it would only be a matter of time before they made the first move, thinking they had the upper-hand while the newcomers were distracted.

Amberly knew what was coming next and she couldn't bring herself to watch as yet another person died at the hands of the Vampires. Not when the faces of her friends were still fresh in her mind.

Quickly closing her eyes, she turned away and braced herself for the sounds she couldn't drown out. But they never came.

Instead of the awful sucking sounds as the Vampires fed upon the newcomers, all she heard were two loud cracks followed quickly by thuds.

Amberly jump when she felt rough hands pulling at the ropes around her wrist. She looked up to see what was happening and her eyes instantly clashed with the glowing amber eyes of the Shapeshifter.

A moment later another set of hands began untying

her ankles. She didn't need to look down to know the Demon was there.

Shocked at the sudden turn of events, Amberly didn't know what to do.

She couldn't stop her eyes from wondering to where the Vampires now lie dead on floor. Was she going to be next? Was that why they were rescuing her, so they could finish her off themselves?

"Don't worry," the Shapeshifter said in a soothing voice when she tried to pull away. "We're here to help you."

A surge of hope shot through her at his words, but she quickly pushed it away. She'd never heard of monsters helping Humans before, so why would it be different for her?

"We'll have you free in a moment," the Demon told her. "Then we'll get you out of here."

It was only then that she remembered about the Vampire the other two had been waiting for. Whether they were really helping her out of the goodness of their heart or not, they needed to know another Vampire was on the way there.

"His friend," she croaked.

It felt like razor blades were slicing her throat when she tried to speak.

"Don't worry," the Shapeshifter said, not understanding what she meant. "His friend is just as dead as he is."

Shaking her head, she tried again. "No... other friend... on way."

"What?" the Demon asked.

Amberly looked down at him. Panic set in when he stopped untying her ankles.

"Another… friend…" Amberly said again.

Her words came out weaker and weaker each time she spoke. It was obvious she was quickly losing her voice, which wasn't a good thing when she needed it the most.

"Is there more coming?" the Demon asked.

Instead of trying to speak, she just nodded her head.

"How many?" the Shapeshifter asked.

He'd managed to free one of her hands while she'd been trying to explain. So, she used her free hand to hold up a finger, to let them know there was one more on his way.

"We need to be gone," the Demon said as he looked at his friend. "Like, now!"

"Yeah, I know," he agreed.

Without another word, both of them ripped the last of the rope apart like it was nothing.

Before she had a chance to move, the Shapeshifter wrapped her in a blanket and picked her up. Holding her in his arms like a mother would hold a baby.

Amberly felt like a child as he held her tightly. What shocked her though, was how safe she felt there.

"I won't drop you, I promise," he said when she stared at him.

She wasn't concerned about him dropping her. His touch was incredibly gentle, but there was no mistaking how strong he was.

She didn't trust her voice to work, so she nodded at him before closing her eyes and tucking her head into his neck.

Amberly couldn't help but take in a deep breath through her nose. His scent reminded her of sandalwood and jasmine.

The last time someone held her like that had been when her mother was alive. Many years had passed since then.

Even though Amberly had to grow up fast after losing her mother at a young age, she'd always had Natalia and Donovan by her side. The three of them had always been more like siblings than friends.

Amberly's heart hurt at the loss of her friends, especially Donovan. She'd never see his happy face again. Never be able to hug him when she's had a bad day. Never laugh at his silly antics.

Tears threatened to escape at thoughts of Donovan, so she pushed them to the back of her mind. She would not break down in front of the monsters, even if they were helping her.

She didn't know if she'd ever see Natalia again, but she held out hope that she would. She didn't want to leave without knowing if Natalia was there or not, but she couldn't ask her rescuers to risk their lives on the off chance that she was.

Maybe when she was stronger, she'd be able to search for Natalia on her own. Not that she'd be able to save her from the monsters by herself. She was more likely to get herself caught again.

Sometimes, she really hated being a Human. Compared to the other species, they were nothing... less than nothing. It was no wonder the other species were hell bent on killing every last one of them.

Not only were they the weakest of the bunch, they were also responsible for the extinction of so many species of animal and plant life on the planet. From what she'd read in books, the planet had been a lush fertile land until Humans came alone and destroyed it.

So, she didn't blame the monsters, but she did wish they'd give Humans a second chance. Just because their ancestors had acted in such a way, it didn't mean that it would be the same for the rest of them.

Amberly for one had more respect for nature than her ancestors had, and so did everyone else she knew.

Had known, she reminded herself.

She didn't see the monsters giving Humans another chance anytime soon. But then, she never thought she'd be rescued from the monsters by other monsters either. So, anything was possible.

She just had to hold out hope for a better future, even if it's one without her in it.

Chapter 8

Dain hung back while Taredd made sure the coast was clear before leaving the tent. It was even more imperative they made a clean getaway now they had Amberly with them.

She couldn't fight the Vampires, and while he was carrying her, he couldn't either. So, the last thing they needed was to bump into anyone on their way out of the tent.

"Wait here," Taredd whispered before ducking out of the tent.

Dain hated having to rely on others to fight for him. He would much rather be the one to fight if need be, but at that moment in time, he was more than willing to let Taredd do it for him.

There was something about Amberly that brought out

his protective instincts. It was more than just because she was Natalia's friend. It was something deeper, more primal.

He knew Taredd would be more than happy to carry her for him, but he didn't want anyone near her. Especially while she was only covered by a blanket.

Just the thought of another male seeing her naked body set his blood on fire and made him want to rip them to shreds.

Dain refused to look too deeply into why she brought out those feelings in him. He needed to concentrate on getting them out of the Vampire camp unseen, and he couldn't do that if he was thinking about her.

It wasn't long before Taredd returned and gave the all clear. Dain quickly followed him outside.

Snaking their way between the tents, they kept to the shadows as best they could. Ducking down low whenever they heard a noise.

It was only a matter of time before the two dead Vampires were found, especially if Amberly was right about them expecting another one to turn up. And when that happened, they would have the entire horde of Vampires after them.

One thing about Vampires; they didn't take kindly to other species stealing their prisoners, their food. And they wouldn't relinquish them without a fight.

The longer they were roaming around the campsite, the more chance there was of them being seen. As it was, they had taken a massive risk just entering the Vampire's camp. They definitely didn't want to get caught stealing from them as well. That was just asking for trouble.

Thankfully, they were able to make it to the woods without being seen, but it still didn't mean they got away Scott-free.

As soon as they were engulfed in darkness by the surrounding woodland, they picked up speed. Instead of heading straight for their own camp and Natalia, they headed in the opposite direction just in case anyone was following them.

Zigzagging their way through the woods, they crossed a river several times before finally heading back to where they'd left Natalia.

Thankfully, they didn't run into any Vampires lurking in the area, or any other species for that matter.

It wasn't just Vampires they had to keep an eye out for. There was no telling what other species were wondering around the woods.

It took them longer than it should have to make it back, but they wanted to make it harder for the Vampires to follow them. Or at least give themselves enough time to get back, pack up, and hit the road again.

Even though their camp wasn't anywhere close to the Vampires, it was still too close for Dain's comfort.

Natalia was still where they'd left her, sat around the small fire. She spun around when she heard them approaching through the woods.

"It's just us," Taredd assured her.

"Thank god you're back," she said. "I was starting to worry. You've been gone for ages. Did everything go okay?"

"Everything went well," Taredd told her.

At hearing Natalia's voice, Amberly stirred in his arms. She had been so still and quiet on their way back, he thought she'd fallen asleep.

"Nat?" she whispered as she turned to look for her friend.

"Amberly!" Natalia squealed.

Amberly nodded her head as tears began to streak down her face. When Dain looked up at Natalia, he noticed she was crying as well.

"I can't believe it's you," Natalia said as she rushed over to them.

Amberly flinched in his arms as Natalia went to reach out and touch her. She must have noticed the movement because she stopped short, her arms falling lifelessly to her sides as sadness filled her eyes.

"You too," Amberly said as she smiled weakly.

He could tell neither female knew what to say or do next. So, he decided it would be the perfect time to clean up and dress Amberly's wounds and find her some clothing to put on.

He really did not like the idea of anyone other than him seeing her naked body. The sooner she had clothes on, the better it would be for his own sanity.

"Well, you two can catch up in a bit," he told them. "But first, I need to see to Amberly's wounds and find her something to wear."

She looked up in surprise when he said her name.

"Oh, god," Natalia gasped. "You're hurt!"

"Don't worry," Dain said, answering so Amberly didn't have to strain her voice again as she tried to speak. "She'll be okay."

"Don't worry, my love," Taredd said as he gently guided her back to the fire. "She's in good hands with Dain."

"Okay," she said, looking back over her shoulder at Amberly.

Dain could see Natalia wanted to help, but there really wasn't anything she could do. Unfortunately, only time could heal most of the damage done to Amberly.

With a little help from the balms and tinctures he carried with him; her physical wounds should be healed within a few days… a week at most. It was the emotional wounds that were going to take the longest to heal.

As he turned around and began walking towards the cart, he heard Amberly whisper 'thank you' to him.

"You're welcome," he whispered back. "If you ever need to talk about it, we're all here for you."

He knew what she must have been through, he'd seen it in the past. The worse thing she could do is lock it all up inside her. It would slowly eat away at her.

When she was ready to talk about what she'd gone through, he wanted her to know she wasn't alone and could open up to them. That there were still people there for her, that cared about her, and not only Natalia.

She might not want her friend to know what she had been through, so it was important she knew there were other options.

Even knowing what she had more than likely gone

through, neither he nor Taredd would say a thing to Natalia. It wasn't their place. Only Amberly could decide if she wanted her to know.

The cart was set a little away from the fire. It wasn't much privacy, but it was better than nothing.

The bedroll was already laid out in the back of the cart. It wasn't perfect, but it was a lot more comfortable than the hard wood.

Dain assumed Taredd had done it for Natalia before they left, in case she wanted to get some sleep while they were gone.

He gently lowered Amberly onto the bedroll, being careful to keep the blanket around her. Not that she was going to be able to keep it while he saw to her injuries.

"I'm sorry," he said. "But I need to check your wounds and apply antiseptic cream, otherwise you might get an infection. It will sting, but I'll do my best not to hurt you."

"I know," she croaked. "Just do what you need to."

"If you feel uncomfortable or are in a lot of pain at any point, just say and we can stop," he assured her.

After everything she'd been through already, the last thing he wanted was to cause her more discomfort or pain, but it was the only way to deal with her wounds to prevent an infection. It would take a lot longer to heal, plus she could become extremely ill if left untreated.

"It's okay," she croaked. "I understand."

"I'll try to be as quick and gentle as possible," he said.

This time she nodded her head in answer.

Dain grabbed his bag of tricks from the front of the

cart and then returned to her side. He pulled out a clean cloth and antiseptic cream before unwrapping the blanket from around her.

Using the water from his canister, he gently began cleaning her wounds.

Seeing all the cuts and bruises marring her perfect body made him so angry. He couldn't help grinding his teeth as he seethed.

It took all of his willpower not to march back to the Vampire campsite and kill them all. The only thing that stopped him was the fact Amberly needed him in that moment.

"By the way, I'm Dain," he introduced himself after realising she still didn't know who he was. "And the red dude over there is Taredd."

"Thank you for rescuing me," she whispered.

"You're more than welcome," he said, smiling warmly.

Other than flinching occasionally, Amberly didn't give any indication that he was hurting her. Even as he applied the antiseptic cream, she barely made a sound.

Brave little thing.

He knew first-hand the cream stung like a bitch. He hated having it applied and would bitch and moan the entire time. So, she was taking it a hell of a lot better than he would.

"All done," he finally said. "The stinging should go down soon, and I've got something to help with your throat as well.

He wrapped the blanket back around her so she could

start warming up while he found some clothes for her to wear.

"Thank you," she croaked.

"But first," he said, smiling. "Let's get you dressed and settled by the fire so you can warm up. It's not the warmest of nights."

Amberly gave him a small smile in return. "Sounds good."

He didn't think Natalia would mind sharing the clothes he'd picked up for her with Amberly, so he picked out a couple of items for her. Luckily, they were both about the same size.

Once she was dressed, Dain picked her up and carried her over to the fire. He gently placed her on the floor opposite Natalia and Taredd before returning for a clean blanket.

He refused to let her use the same one they'd taken from the Vampires. Instead, he hid it from view so she wouldn't be reminded of her time with them.

"Thank you," she whispered when he placed the clean blanket over her shoulders.

"You're welcome," he told her before returning to the cart to get a drink for her throat.

"It's so good to see you," he heard Natalia say.

"You too," Amberly said faintly.

"I didn't think I'd see anyone from our group ever again," Natalia said. "Especially after seeing the carnage in the bunker."

After mixing some herbs in a cup of hot water, he joined Amberly on the floor opposite the others. He handed her the drink as he sat down next to her.

"Thank you," she said.

She was still shivering, so he crossed his legs and lifted her onto his lap. Tucking the blanket tightly around her, he made sure her hands were free before wrapping his arms around her waist to share his warmth.

Dain expected her to pull away, but she didn't. Instead, she nestled into his arms, and even let out a contented sigh.

Taredd watched them closely, but didn't say a word.

"Better?" he asked when she placed the empty cup on the floor.

"Yes, thank you," she said, sounding better already.

"You're welcome," he told her.

"I know you probably don't want to talk about it yet," Natalia spoke softly. "But I need to know what happened?"

"It's okay," Amberly said. "Bella's what happened. She showed the Vampires where we were. She brought them right to the door."

"That bitch," Natalia spat. "No wonder I couldn't find her. You wait until I get my hands on her."

"You're too late," Amberly said. "She's already got her comeuppance. The Vampires made sure of that."

"Good," Natalia said. "She deserved everything she got."

Dain didn't know who Bella was, but he agreed with Natalia. It was a good job she wasn't still around.

"What about Donovan?" Natalia asked. "Is he still alive?"

Sadness surrounded Amberly at the mention of the name. She tensed up in his arms as Dain could feel it in her body, and he could smell it as it seeped from her pores.

Whoever Donovan was, he meant an awful lot to Amberly.

"He didn't make it," Amberly said as tears slid down her cheeks. "None of them made it. Only me."

So why did they keep her alive?

It made absolutely no sense to Dain. Why would they kill all the others and keep Amberly alive? What was so special about her that they decided to spare her life?

It couldn't be because they wanted to use her body and keep her as a food supply, but that was the only thing he could think of. There was no other reason why they wouldn't drain her dry and dump her dead body at their feet.

There had to be a reason behind it, he just couldn't think what it might be. It certainly wasn't out of the goodness of their hearts.

No, they had a plan for Amberly, he just didn't know what it was.

He could tell Taredd was trying to wrap his head around it as well. There was something off about the entire situation that neither he nor Taredd could figure out.

Unfortunately, it meant Dain and Taredd had probably interrupted whatever plans they had. Which meant it was even more likely the Vampires were going to come after her.

"Are you sure?" Natalia asked.

Amberly shivered in his arms, but this time it wasn't from the cold. No doubt it was from the memories of what she'd witnessed. He could imagine what she'd been made to watch.

"No," she said, shaking her head. "There's no chance any of them survived. I was there when they died. I was made to watch."

Dain tightened his hold on her, comforting her the only way he knew how. If he could, he'd take away her memories from that time, but unfortunately, he couldn't.

Natalia didn't make a sound, but he could see tears streaming down her cheeks.

"I'm sorry," Taredd said, breaking the silence that formed around them as Natalia and Amberly mourned their friends. "But we really need to get going."

Natalia wiped the tears from her cheeks before looking over her shoulder at Taredd.

"Why?" Natalia asked.

He kissed her on the forehead before replying. "Unfortunately, it's only a matter of time before the two Vampires' we killed are discovered. When that happens, the rest of them will come looking for those responsible."

If they hadn't already been, Dain thought.

"I thought we'd be safe here since it's not near their camp," Natalia said. "Isn't that why we stopped here?"

"No, it was only going to be a temporary stop while we rescued your friend," he explained. "It's not safe to stay for too long because we're too close to their camp. It won't take them long to find us when they start looking. So, we need to make a move sooner rather than later."

Which was why they had taken the long way back and crossed a river several times. They hadn't done it just for the hell of it. They were giving themselves more time to leave the area before the Vampires caught up with them.

"Taredd's right," Dain said. "It's not safe enough here. So the sooner we get going, the better." He rubbed a hand over his face. "I'm surprised they haven't come looking already."

"So am I," Taredd said. "It's not worth the risk of staying longer."

"Why did you get the bed set up before you left then?" Natalia asked. "Wouldn't it have been easier to leave it all packed away until we get to where we're going?"

"I set it up in case you wanted to rest while we were gone," Taredd told her. "And just in case it was needed when we got back."

"Ah, I see," she said. "So, do we need to pack it all away again?"

"No," Taredd said. "We'll leave it for now. If you or Amberly want to sleep along the way, then you can do."

"I'm not sure I'll be able to sleep," Natalia said, covering a yawn with the back of her hand. "It gets a bit bumpy in the back."

"I'm sure you'll be able to if you get tired enough," Taredd said as he lifted her to her feet.

Dain did the same with Amberly. She pulled the blanket tighter around herself as she watched Natalia and Taredd move around the fire.

"Yeah, you might be right," she said. "We'll see."

"Just don't start snoring again," Dain said. "Otherwise, you'll definitely get us caught."

"I don't snore," she said adamantly.

Amberly giggled. It was only a slight sound, yet it set his blood racing.

It amazed him she was able to find joy so soon after everything she'd been through. He just wished it hadn't been so fleeting.

Dain wanted to hear the sound again. He didn't care what it took; he swore he'd make her giggle, even if it killed him.

Chapter 9

Amberly wasn't sure what to make of the situation she found herself in.

On the one hand, she was over the moon that Natalia was still alive. But on the other hand, it looked like Natalia had aligned herself with the monsters.

Admittedly, the Shapeshifter and Demon Natalia was with seemed to be a hell of a lot better than the Vampires Bella had mixed with. And at least with Natalia, Amberly wasn't tied to a makeshift bed while Vampires used her body and drank her blood.

She shuddered at the memory, and Dain tightened his arms around her. Yeah, she much preferred the Shapeshifter and Demon over the Vampires.

She was even more surprised when Dain tended to her wounds. She hadn't been prepared for such a gentle touch from a Shapeshifter, but then, she hadn't been prepared for the physical attraction she had towards him either.

The antiseptic cream stung like a bitch, but the warmth of his hands made it more bearable. She hadn't expected much from the drink he'd given her, but she had to admit, her throat was feeling a lot better.

It didn't feel like razor blades were slicing her throat to pieces every time she spoke.

She couldn't stop the giggle from escaping when Dain pointed out that Natalia snored. Amberly had known for years, but whenever she pointed it out, everyone else would say she was hearing things.

It was nice to know she wasn't the only one that heard it, but it would have been better if it was another Human that noticed. Obviously, Dain and Taredd would be able to hear her, they were monsters after all. They would probably be able to hear a pin drop.

Watching the way Natalia and Taredd were with each other, it was obvious something was going on between them. She'd never seen Natalia so comfortable around a male before.

She didn't argue, fight, or push away from him when he picked her up and start carrying her over to the cart. Amberly was about to follow them when she was suddenly swept off her feet.

Next thing she knew, Dain was carrying her over to the cart again.

"I can walk," she told him.

"Yeah, I know," he said, but he still didn't put her

down.

"You can put me down," she said.

"I will when we get to the cart," he said.

Amberly gave up. She was too exhausted to argue with him. Plus, she kind of liked the feel of his strong arms around her, holding her tight. Not to mention there wasn't much she could do to stop him.

Even on her best day, she didn't have the strength to fight him, and it was far from her best day. Just holding the cup while she drank was more difficult than it should have been.

She was surprised Natalia was trusting them. She hated their kind as much as Amberly. Or at least, she used to.

With his long strides, it didn't take Dain long to cover the distance between the fire and the cart. He gently sat her on the edge, making sure she was firmly on before letting go of her.

"Shuffle up to the other end," he told her. "It can get pretty bumpy in the back and we don't want you bouncing off."

Without saying a word, she did as he said and was rewarded with a smile. She watched as he turned around and walked back over to the fire.

"Are you okay?" Natalia asked, making Amberly jump.

She was so absorbed in watching Dain move around in the firelight; she hadn't noticed Natalia sit down next to her on the cart.

"Um… yeah, I'm okay," she said, glancing away

from him.

There was something about him that intrigued her, it drew her attention like a magnet. His eyes, the way he moved, his gentle touch, it all attracted her, but there was something else as well.

Yes, he'd rescued her from the Vampires. And yes, he'd seen to her wounds and shown her kindness. But could that really be all it was? She didn't know, and she wasn't ready to look too deeply into it either.

"I'm sorry about what happened to you," Natalia said.

"It wasn't your fault," Amberly told her. "Nobody could have known what Bella was going to do, least of all you."

Which was true. Nobody could have guessed what Bella would do. Nobody could have foreseen her selling out the rest of them just to save her own skin. Not that it worked out too well for her in the end.

She deserved what she got.

Amberly refused to feel sorry for the woman, or mourn her like the others, because if it hadn't been for her, none of them would have died.

"I know, but I shouldn't have left to go looking for her," she said. "I should have been with you."

"There's nothing you could have done that would've change the outcome," Amberly told her. "In fact, you would have been caught as well. You might not have been as lucky as I was."

"Were you lucky?" Natalia asked.

"I'm alive, aren't I?" Amberly asked.

Guilt ate at her. She was lucky to be alive, but deep

down, she didn't feel lucky. Everyone she'd known and loved were all gone. The only person she had left was Natalia, but she was different now.

Amberly didn't know what happened to Natalia while she'd been away, but the old Natalia wouldn't have cozied up with the monsters. Any of them.

"Yes, you're alive," Natalia agreed. "And you're free."

Amberly wasn't so sure about the free part. Only time would tell if she was truly free, or if she'd traded one prison for another.

She hoped Natalia was right, but after everything she'd been through recently, she was going to need a bit more convincing. Until then, she'd hold out judgment.

Dain kicked dirt over the fire, encasing them in darkness once more. Amberly welcomed the darkness. She didn't need to try so hard to keep a brave face because Natalia wouldn't be able to see it slip.

It only took a moment for Amberly's eyes to adjust to the darkness. Along with having better hearing than Natalia and everyone else she'd known, she also had better eyesight, especially at night.

Amberly learnt at a young age to keep what she could do a secret. Her mother knew, but nobody else did.

She knew what they would have thought if they'd ever found out. They would have questioned whether or not she was actually a Human.

Admittedly, she asked her mother that same question when she was younger. There were so many differences between her and the other children she grew up with, it made her wonder if she really was Human, but her mother had assured her she was.

"We'll be leaving in just a minute," Dain said as he tossed a bag in the back with them.

His glowing amber eyes seemed to swirl in the darkness, hypnotizing her. They were such an incredible colour; she couldn't take her eyes off them.

Natalia could barely see her hand in front of her face. She was waving it around in front of her.

Monsters didn't have that problem, so Dain and Taredd would be able to see as easily as Amberly could in the darkness, if not better.

"It's a good job they can see in the dark," Natalia said. "Because I can't see a bloody thing."

It was also the reason Amberly and Natalia hadn't been able to enjoy looking up at the stars when they were growing up. They couldn't see as well as the monsters in the dark, so it was too dangerous to wonder around after night had fallen.

Amberly had never told anyone, but there were many times she'd ignored the rules and gone outside at night. And not just when she was a child either.

The call of the moon and stars was too much for her to resist. So, whenever she got the opportunity, she would sneak out after everyone else had gone to sleep.

It didn't matter what season it was; she enjoyed her night time walks. It was so incredibly peaceful at night.

Whether she was lying down in the middle of a field looking up at the stars, swimming in a lake as deep and dark as the night sky, or walking barefoot among ancient woodland, she loved every minute of her freedom. She never felt more alive than when she was surrounded by nature.

Amberly knew none of them would understand her need to be one with nature, so she never told any of them about it. They would all call her insane for needing to feel the earth beneath her feet. Not even Natalia knew about her night-time activities, or her need to be one with nature.

She was jolted out of her thoughts as the cart began moving.

"It's bumpy as hell," Natalia said. "But it's better than walking."

"I noticed," Amberly said.

To be honest, she would much rather be walking. She hadn't been able to stretch her legs in days, and it had been even longer since she last walked barefoot.

"Where are they taking us?" Amberly finally plucked up the courage to ask.

"I'm not sure where we're going," Natalia said. "But don't worry, they'll keep us safe."

Amberly wasn't so sure about that, but she didn't comment. She would hold out judgment until she knew a little more about them.

Normally, she would trust Natalia unconditionally, but things were different now. Bella had sold her and the others out to the monsters, and now Natalia had joined forces with them.

Amberly didn't know how she was supposed to feel about Dain and Taredd at that moment, and she didn't want to think about it either. Her head was banging, she was exhausted, and she was starving. Not to mention the bad smell that was emanating from her.

Never in her life had she smelt so bad, but it wasn't like she had a choice in the matter. Being tied down for days had taken that choice away from her.

The first chance she got; she was going to scrub every inch of her body until it was red raw.

"I'm going to lie down for a while," Amberly said. "I'm absolutely shattered."

She was exhausted, but that wasn't the main reason why she wanted to lie down.

She didn't know what to talk to Natalia about. It was the first time in her life that she couldn't think of anything to talk to her best friend about.

She'd never been able to act as if nothing was wrong, and definitely not with Natalia. She had always been able to read Amberly like a book. So, it wouldn't take long for her to realise something was wrong with her.

Since Amberly didn't want to lie to Natalia, she thought it would be best if she just pretended to be asleep for a while. At least until she could think things through.

It wasn't exactly the easiest place to fall asleep, even if she really wanted to. She could feel every single bump, but at least she had time to think.

Her mind whirled with everything that happened since she'd last seen Natalia. Everything that happened with Bella, what the monsters put her through, and everything since she'd been rescued.

As much as she didn't want to admit it, Dain and Taredd were nothing like any of the other monsters she'd dealt with so far. Dain in particular was nothing like she thought he would be.

"I'm going to get some sleep as well," she heard Natalia say a few minutes later.

"Okay," Taredd said. "We'll wake you when we stop."

"I don't think you'll have to wake me," she said. "Not unless the ground suddenly becomes smooth, but I'm going to try anyway."

"Sorry," Dain said. "I don't think that's going to happen."

"Yeah, I didn't think so," she said. "Well, I'm still going to lie down for a bit."

Amberly didn't make a sound as Natalia laid down behind her. She kept her eyes closed and her breathing steady in hopes that Natalia would think she was asleep already.

She would need all the time she could get to prepare herself for tomorrow, because she would not be able to ignore Natalia forever. Or Dain.

Chapter 10

Not willing to risk being caught by the Vampires, they didn't stop until the sun was rising. And only for a short time.

There was no telling how close the Vampires were behind them. Dain didn't doubt they were being tracked down. For some reason, they had kept Amberly alive, so they weren't going to just let her go.

Natalia dozed off at one point when the ground evened out a little, but it wasn't long before she was woken again. She cried out as her head made impact with the side of the cart when it went over a hidden ditch.

Taredd had pulled the horse to a stop so he could make sure she was okay, and then they were back on their way.

Years ago, before the Great war, the Humans used to

cover the ground with tarmac to smooth out the roads they created. Most had been destroyed in the war, and the rest were taken back by nature, leaving nothing but uneven ground in its wake.

He was positive Amberly hadn't slept at all, even though she hadn't made a sound for hours and had barely moved. Admittedly, he wouldn't be able to sleep in the back of the cart either.

Dain would much rather sleep on the cold, hard ground than in the back of a moving cart. Well, if he was being completely honest, he would much rather be sleeping in his own bed.

He couldn't remember the last time he slept in his own bed. It had been far too long since he was last there. He missed his family.

Okay, maybe not his whole family, but he missed his mother and little sister. He couldn't wait to see them again.

He bet his sister was a right handful now she was grown up. She was only a teenager the last time he saw her. And his mother, he bet she was still just as beautiful as she'd ever been.

That was the great thing about being a Shapeshifter. They didn't age like the Humans did. As soon as they hit maturity, they stopped aging.

He wasn't looking forward to seeing his father again, though. Last he heard; his father was still pissed at him for not taking the Shapeshifters side in the Great war.

It wasn't like he'd chosen a different side or anything. He just refused to fight in a war he didn't agree with.

So instead, he spent his time with Taredd and Arun, which just pissed his father off even more.

Dain was jolted out of his thoughts by Taredd pulling the horse to a halt.

"We'll stop here for a while," he said. "I don't know about you three, but I'm starving."

"Sounds good to me," Natalia said.

"I'm up for food," Dain said.

"When aren't you?" Taredd laughed.

"Ha ha," Dain said sarcastically.

Before he could say anything else, Amberly's stomach rumbled loudly. Everyone turned to look at her.

"Sounds like you could definitely do with something to eat," Taredd said.

"When was the last time you ate anything?" Natalia asked her.

Amberly shrugged her shoulder. "I don't know. A day or two."

Dain knew that wasn't the truth. She wouldn't have eaten anything since before she was captured by the Vampires.

They were more than happy to feed upon their prisoners, but they weren't prepared to return the favour. So, it was unlikely they had given her anything to eat, or drink for that matter.

"Don't worry, we have plenty of food," Dain said. "And even if we run out, Taredd can catch us some more with his traps."

"Yep," Natalia said. "Taredd caught us dinner when we first met."

"Not to mention Dain could catch us something as well," Taredd added. "I'm sure he wouldn't mind turning into an animal to catch us dinner."

Amberly's eyes widened at the mention of him shifting. He didn't know if it was because she was scared, or if she was surprised. He didn't think it was the latter, though.

The last thing Dain wanted Amberly to feel around him was fear. He wanted her to feel safe around him. To know that he was there to look after her, not harm her. So, if that was the case, he needed to rectify it as soon as possible.

"Anyway," Dain said as he jumped down off the cart. "I'm starving, so let's get a fire going so we can have something to eat before we have to get going again."

He walked to the back of the cart and helped Amberly down before grabbing the bag with food in. Amberly didn't complain as he hooked his hands under her arms and lifted her off the cart.

"Thank you," she said quietly.

"You're welcome," he told her.

After Taredd helped Natalia down, the two females moved off to the side and watched as he and Taredd collected what they needed from the back of the cart. When they had everything together, they led the females to a small clearing a little away from the horse and cart.

Taredd dumped the bags on the floor before returning to unhook the horse.

"I'll be back in a few minutes," he said.

"Where's he taking the horse?" Amberly asked.

"To get a drink," Dain told her. "There's a river just over there."

Even though they couldn't see the river, Dain could hear it.

"Oh," Amberly said as she watched Taredd walk away.

He could see she hadn't expected that to be the answer. He didn't know what she expected him to say, but he really hoped she didn't think they were going to eat the horse. Because that was not going to happen.

Yes, they both liked their meat, but horse was definitely off the menu.

"Don't worry," Natalia said. "I can't hear the river either."

"I can hear it," she said, surprising him. "I just didn't know it was where he was going."

They weren't particularly close to the river, so he was amazed she was able to hear it.

He always thought Humans didn't have very good hearing. He could only just pick up the sound and his senses were a hell of a lot better than theirs, even in his Human form.

"I still can't hear a thing," Natalia said a moment later. "But then, you've always had better hearing than anyone I know."

Dain's interest was well and truly piqued. There was something about her, something that made her stand out from all the other Humans he'd come across, including Natalia.

He wanted to know everything there was to know

about her. But he could see that was going to be easier said than done.

He could see it in her eyes, and the way she was around them, that she didn't trust them. And he couldn't blame her.

After everything her kind had gone through over the years, it was completely understandable. Not to mention what she'd just been through with the Vampires.

Dain tried, and failed, to ignore her as he set about preparing the meal. He didn't have to look in Amberly's direction to know where she was or know what she was doing. He could feel her standing behind him, watching his every move.

He didn't blame her for being cautious. He would be the same in her position.

He itched to pull her into his arms and promise her everything would be alright, that she was safe, and that he would give his life to protect hers. But he didn't. There was no point, it would only have the opposite effect.

She didn't know him from Adam. Telling her that she was safe with him wouldn't work. Only showing her would, and that was going to take time.

"Um... can I..." Amberly stuttered as she looked between him and the direction of the river. "Do you mind... if I... um... go wash up?"

"Of course," Dain said. "Just wait until Taredd's back and I'll show you the way."

"It's okay," she said. "I can find my way."

"Are you sure?" he asked.

"Yep, I'm sure," she said.

"I'll go with you," Natalia said. "I can collect some water, and if we're quick, I can get Taredd to help carry it back as well."

Dain wasn't sure it was a good idea to let them go off on their own. He was positive Taredd wouldn't be happy about it either. But he had to admit, it would be helpful if Natalia could collect some water.

He supposed it wasn't too far away, and when they were out of his sight, they should be within Taredd's.

"Okay, I don't see why not," he said.

"Don't worry, we're not going to run off," Natalia said.

He knew she wouldn't run off, but he wasn't so sure about Amberly. From the looks of it, she was waiting for the perfect opportunity to slip away unseen.

Dain really hoped he was wrong. The last thing he wanted was for her to run off and get herself caught by the Vampires again, or any of the other species that were on the hunt for Humans.

"I know you won't," he told her, but he refrained from pointing out that Amberly might.

"Hold on a sec," Natalia told Amberly. "I'll grab you some clean clothes to change into once you've washed."

"Thanks," Amberly said.

"There should be a bar of soap and a clean towel in one of the bags," he told them.

Natalia rummaged around in a bag, grabbing a few items of clothing and putting them in a pile. She handed the clothes along with a towel and bar of soap to Amberly and then she picked up the water bottles before they both headed off towards the river.

"We won't be long," Natalia shouted over her shoulder.

Dain didn't bother answering. He just continued setting up a pile of wood for a fire.

As temped as he was to follow them, he held back. There was no need for him to follow, he could easily hear them, and so he would know if they wondered off. Plus, Taredd was by the river. He would be able to hear them coming, so would keep an eye out for them as well.

No, his time was better spent getting a fire going and sorting out food for everyone. Because the sooner they were back on the road, the better.

They still needed to find Arun, and he was positive the Vampires were hot on their trail.

They kept Amberly alive for a reason, and he had a feeling it wasn't just as food on tap. If he was right, then they weren't going to let her go easily. Which meant they were going to come after her.

Sooner or later, they were going to have a run in with the Vampires. He just hoped Arun was with them before that happened. Having that one extra person on their side would make the world of difference, especially while trying to keep Natalia and Amberly safe.

It wouldn't be such a problem if they didn't have Amberly and Natalia to look out for. But even if the females knew how to fight, they still wouldn't be able to hold their own against the Vampires because they were Human.

Thank God there's only two of them.

He dreaded to think what it would be like if more of their group had survived.

Chapter 11

Amberly could tell by the tone of Dain's voice that he didn't believe she wouldn't run off, and he was right. The first chance she got; she was out of there.

She didn't have a clue where she was going to go, but there was no way in hell she was hanging around with the monsters she'd spent her entire life running from. It just wasn't in her nature.

The only downside was, she would be completely on her own. For the first time in her life, she would have nobody to watch her back and it scared the living shit out of her.

Her heart ached at the thought of being all by herself, but there was no other way. Even without asking, she could tell Natalia would not leave with her.

She didn't know what happened in her absence, but

Natalia wasn't the same person she'd grown up with. For one thing, she seemed smitten with the big red guy.

Amberly didn't know what she saw in Taredd, but it was obvious there was something going on between the two of them. Every time she looked at the Demon, she went all mushy eyed.

"Are you sure you're okay?" Natalia asked when they were alone.

"Yeah, I'm fine," she lied.

She was as far away from fine as she could possibly get, but she couldn't bring herself to tell Natalia. Especially when she seemed so happy.

Not to mention Dain and Taredd would be able to hear their conversation. If Amberly could still hear Dain moving around as he got a fire going, or Taredd talking calmly to the horse as it drank from the river, then they could definitely hear her and Natalia talking.

"You can tell me anything, you know that," Natalia said.

"I know," she said. "But I promise, there's nothing to tell."

"Okay."

Amberly was dying to ask her what was going on between her and Taredd, but she didn't know how to start the conversation. Whatever it was, it appeared to be mutual.

She had to admit, she could kind of see the appeal. Taredd definitely wasn't her type. The red skin and black horns did absolutely nothing for her. But Dain? He was a completely different matter.

The man is a walking sex god! She thought.

Shapeshifters shouldn't be allowed to be that sexy. They just shouldn't. How the hell were Human women supposed to resist creatures that looked like him?

Those glowing amber eyes of his sent butterflies off in her stomach every time they landed on her. And that smile of his? Well, what could she say about that other than it made her knees go weak and her blood race through her body.

She all but melted into a puddle at his feet whenever he aimed that smile at her.

He was dangerous, in more ways than one. But even knowing that, it didn't stop her fingers from itching to trace every dip and curve of his bulging muscles.

The loose fitting t-shirt and trousers did little to hide the size of him. Amberly doubted she'd be able to reach her arms all the way around his chest, it was so large. That didn't mean she wasn't willing to give it a try though, which confused the hell out of her.

She should fear his kind, not lust after them.

"I promise, these are the good guys, Amberly," Natalia said a moment later. "Neither of them will hurt us."

"No, Natalia, they're not the good guys," Amberly said. "It's plan to see that they're not. One's a Shapeshifter, for fuck's sake, and the other is a Demon. Neither of which had been very kind to our species in the past. So, what makes you think they will be any different?"

She didn't bother keeping her voice low, there was no point. Both of them could easily hear them, even if they whispered. Which, in Amberly's eyes, was a completely unfair advantage.

Yes, she had good hearing, but it was nothing compared to theirs.

"I know you'll find it hard to believe after everything you've been through…"

"Don't you mean after everything we've all been through?" she pointed out.

Because she certainly hadn't been the only one to suffer over the years, they all had. The entire Human race had suffered at the hands of the monsters, not just her.

"Yes, we've all suffered," Natalia agreed. "But that doesn't mean I'm wrong about those two. I've never led us wrong before, have I?"

"Um, yes," Amberly said. "When you decided we were heading north. When you decided to leave us to go looking for Bella."

Amberly knew she was in the wrong for throwing Bella in her face. Natalia couldn't have known what was going to happen. She was in the dark just as much as everyone else had been.

"Hey, I wasn't the only one that wanted to head north," she snapped. "Everyone voted, even you. The only person who didn't vote to come this way was Bella."

"Yeah, and look where that got her."

Maybe heading north was a mistake. Maybe Bella was right in saying it was a bad idea. But they couldn't turn back the clocks. They couldn't change what had already been done.

Their friends were gone, and no amount of arguing would change that fact. As her mother always used to say, there's no point looking back because you're not going that way.

All they could do was make the best of what little future they may have left. Amberly certainly didn't want to spend that time arguing with Natalia, or anyone else.

"If she hadn't fucked off and left us, I wouldn't have left you," Natalia said, softening her voice with each word. "I'm sorry for everything that happened, Amberly. I wish I could turn back the clock and do things differently, but I can't. All I can do, is work with what I've got. I can promise you until I'm blue in the face that Taredd and Dain are different, and that we're safe with them. But until you see for yourself, you're not going to believe me."

Natalia was right. It was going to take more than words to prove they were the good guys. Rescuing her from the Vampires had made a start, but she was still a long way off trusting them completely with her life.

"Can you at least give them a chance? For me?" Natalia begged.

Amberly knew Taredd and Dain were listening to their every word, so she couldn't exactly say no. But more than that, after everything they had been through together, how could she possibly say no to Natalia?

"Fine," she gave in. "I'll give them a chance. But if they make one wrong move, I'm out of there."

Natalia squealed with excitement. "I promise, you won't regret it."

She hoped not, for Natalia's sake, but only time would tell.

"Hey, Taredd," Natalia greeted as she bounced over to him. "We've come to collect some water. Can you give us a hand carrying it back?"

"Of course," he said.

He wrapped an arm around her waist and pulled her to his body. Natalia went willingly into his arms. She beamed up at him when he kissed her on the forehead.

"Thank you," she said, smiling.

"Anything for you, my love," he said, smiling back at her.

It was wonderful seeing Natalia so happy, but at the same time, Amberly couldn't help worrying about her. The last thing she wanted was for Taredd and Dain to turn on them, but she couldn't stop the feeling that something bad was going to happen.

Amberly turned away from the couple and found a safe place to put the clean clothes and towel where they wouldn't get wet. She kicked off her shoes and then sat down to take her socks off.

She rolled up the trousers legs as far as they would go before standing up and wading into the water.

Bending down, she scooped up water with her hands and splashed it on her face.

"Amberly," Natalia called from behind her, making her jump.

"Yep," she replied.

Natalia waited until Amberly turned to face her before she continued.

"We're going to head back to camp now. We've filled up the water bottles," she said. "So, if you want to have a proper wash in the river, you don't need to worry about us seeing you."

Thank god!

She had hoped they would leave her alone so she could wash properly. She needed to get the stench of vampire off her body, and the only way she could do that would be by stripping down and fully submerging in the water before scrubbing her hair and body.

She certainly would not be able to get rid of the smell by waddling in the water with her trousers rolled up to her knees.

"Okay, thanks," she said as she headed back to the riverbank.

"You sure you're not going to run off?" Natalia asked when she reach her.

"Yes," she said. "I promised not to run off, so I won't."

Natalia scrutinized Amberly for a moment before nodding her head. "Okay, I'll see you back at camp."

Amberly smiled. "I won't be long, don't worry."

"If you need any help, just shout," Taredd said. "Dain and I will be able to hear you and we'll come running."

Amberly had to admit, it was nice of him to say that, and it made her feel slightly better about being by herself.

"Will do," she said.

"Do you want me to stay with you?" Natalia asked.

"No," Amberly said. "I'll be fine on my own." When they still didn't leave, she added. "I promise, Natalia, I'm not going anywhere. And I promise, the first sign of trouble, and I'll be screaming at the top of my voice."

"Okay," Natalia said. "We'll see you back at camp."

"Yep, see you back there," Amberly said. "I won't be too long."

Natalia nodded her head, but didn't say another word. Along with Taredd and the horse, she headed back to camp, leaving Amberly on her own by the river.

As soon as they disappeared from view, Amberly stripped out of the clothes and waded back into the river. This time she didn't stop until the water was up to her shoulders.

She breathed a sigh of relief as the water flowed downstream, taking the dirt and grime with it.

Amberly pictured the water taking away her troubles with it, lifting a weight off her shoulders at the same time.

She leaned her head back into the water and ran her fingers through her hair. She did her best to wash away the dirt, but it wasn't easy without soap. Then she re-membered Natalia had given her some with the towel.

She made her way back to shore to grab the soap. Before she waded in to her shoulders again, she dipped the soap into the water and scrubbed her hair and body.

When she was done, she threw the soap towards the pile of clean clothes and then walked back into the water.

Soap was a luxury that few Humans had access to anymore. It wasn't like they could pop to the shop like they used to in the old days. So, if they didn't know how to make it, or know somebody that did, they had to go without.

Thankfully, her mother had shown her how to make a simple soap before she died, otherwise she'd probably smell as bad as some of the people that used to be in their group.

She did debate on teaching them how to make their own, but she never got round to it, and now she never would.

Her heart ached at the loss of her friends, especially Donovan. He'd always been her rock, her best friend, her confidant when Natalia wasn't around. She loved him dearly, but only as a sister would love a brother and nothing more.

As much as she wanted to return the feeling he'd had for her, she couldn't. It wasn't through lack of trying either.

He'd been an attractive man. Any woman would have been lucky to have him. Unfortunately, he only had eyes for her.

She never encouraged his affection. She'd always told him nothing would happen between them, but he'd been adamant that one day she'd change her mind.

Amberly sighed as she leaned her head back in the water to rinse the soap. There was nothing she could have done to change his mind, and now it was too late. He was gone forever.

The feelings she'd so desperately prayed to have for Donovan, she now found herself feeling for someone entirely different. A Shapeshifter.

She didn't know what it was about Dain, but he drew her attention like nobody else had ever done before.

117

Even when she wasn't near him, she couldn't stop thinking about him.

Amberly had to admit, she was kind of disturbed by the thoughts swimming around in her mind. She was by no means innocent, but even she was blushing at the images that were floating around in her mind.

She shouldn't be embarrassed by her thoughts. It wasn't like anyone else could see them, but she was.

Amberly didn't know how long she'd been lying back in the river, looking up at the sky. It was so peaceful watching the clouds pass over as she leaned her head back into the water, she didn't want to leave. But she knew if she didn't return soon, Natalia would worry about her.

It wouldn't surprise her if Natalia turned up at the river again. She'd never liked the idea of Amberly being out on her own, so she certainly wouldn't like the idea of her being on her own by the river for too long.

Deciding it was about time she re-joined the others, she lifted her head up and splashed water on her face. When she was done, she turned towards the shore where she'd left the clothes and came face to face with Dain.

She froze, unsure what to do. She couldn't stay in the river forever, but she couldn't leave without him seeing her naked body.

The water was so clear, he could probably see she wasn't wearing anything. Not to mention the discarded clothes she'd been wearing earlier were in a pile right next to the clean ones.

Fuck!

For a split second she wondered how long he'd been stood there, but it was quickly chased away by indecent thoughts of them together. Images flashed in her mind, showing her all the things she wanted to do with him.

Her cheeks burned as she blushed at the indecent images, but she didn't stop them. She couldn't.

It didn't help with the way Dain was staring at her. He looked ready to devour her any second. But what concerned her more, was that she wanted him to... needed him to.

It was like an itch she needed to scratch, and the only person who could do it, was Dain.

Before she knew what she was doing, she was heading towards the shore. Towards Dain.

His eyes stayed locked with hers as she walked out of the river and over to him. She didn't stop until they were inches from each other. Her heart raced so fast; she was sure it was about to burst from her chest.

The hunger in his eyes sent butterflies off in her stomach and moisture to pool between her legs.

Dain didn't say a word as he closed the gap between them. He ran his fingers through her hair, fisting it gently at the back. When she didn't attempt to pull away, he lowered his head and slowly brushed his lips against hers.

Amberly's legs turned to jelly at the delicate touch of his lips. A moment later, she felt his other hand on her back as he pulled her against him.

She melted into his arms at the feel of his rock hard body pressed tightly up against hers. It may be the biggest mistake in the world, but Amberly wanted him inside her, filling her up until she couldn't take anymore.

After everything she'd been through, she needed to feel alive. To feel something other than pain and grief.

But more than anything else, she needed him… needed Dain.

Chapter 12

The last thing he expected to see as he approached the river was Amberly floating around as if she didn't have a care in the world.

Her hair fanned around her like a fiery halo. Her porcelain skin, marred only by a sprinkling of freckles across the bridge of her nose, glistened in the sunlight.

Dain could feel his cock growing as he watched her. He took in every little detail he could and stored it away in his memory. She seemed so relaxed and at peace. He didn't want to disturb her, but he couldn't bring himself to walk away either.

So, he stood frozen in place watching her, waiting for her to notice he was there.

He half expected her to be long gone, not watching the clouds. But that wasn't what surprised him.

As she stood up and looked towards the shore, instead of screaming or trying to cover herself, she stared at him for a moment before boldly walking out of the river. She kept her eyes locked with his as she strolled out of the water and over to him, stopping inches from him.

Her hair was slicked back from her face, and the dirt and grime that covered her was gone, leaving nothing but porcelain skin on show.

Her pert breasts bobbed as she sauntered towards him.

At first, he thought he was imagining everything. It wouldn't be the first time he imagined her doing something like that. It was only when she stopped inches away that he knew his mind wasn't playing tricks on him.

The desire he felt was reflected back at him from her big, beautiful blue eyes. As much as he told himself it was a bad idea, he couldn't stop his feet from moving forward, closing the gap between them.

Running his hand through fiery locks, he fisted his hand at the back of her head and angled her face up to his. When she didn't pull away, he lowered his head and gently brushed his lips against hers.

Amberly instantly opened her mouth for him. He wrapped his other arm around her waist and pulled her against his body. The soft feel of her curves pressed up against his body sent his blood rushing south faster than it had ever done before.

She melted in his arms as he deepened the kiss, setting his blood on fire. She consumed his mind, chasing everything else away until there was nothing left but her.

Taredd and Natalia, Arun, the Vampires, it all faded into nothing. The only thing that mattered in that moment was the female in his arms. Everything else was pushed to the back of his mind.

He couldn't stop the moan from escaping as their tongues twirled together. Especially when Amberly ran her hands through his hair, pulling him closer to her.

Dain released the back of her head so he could run his hands over her wet body. Watching her walk out of the river, water running down her body, was one of the sexiest things he'd ever seen. He'd been with his fair share of females, but none had consumed his entire being the way she did.

He couldn't get close enough to her. He needed to feel her skin against his without the barrier of his clothes in the way.

The image of her naked body was etched into his mind, but he still wanted more. He wanted to learn every dip and curve of her body. Everything that made her moan with pleasure.

He wanted... needed... to hear her cry out his name as she climaxed. It was a burning ache that wouldn't go away.

The only thing separating them was his clothes, but not for long. Amberly was already lifting his t-shirt as her hands snaked their way up his back.

Dain broke the kiss long enough to whip it over his head, and then he was right back to where he'd left off.

Amberly moaned into his mouth at the feel of skin

on skin. The sound sent blood rushing straight to his already straining cock.

Grabbing her ass, he lifted her up. She instantly wrapped her legs around his waist, opening herself up to him.

The feel of her moist lips against his stomach drove him wild. He wanted to be inside her already, but even though she was wet, she wasn't ready for him. Which was why he hadn't taken off his trousers as well.

He knew without a doubt, once his cock was free from the confines of his trousers, he wouldn't be able to stop himself from sliding inside her, whether she was ready or not. So, he didn't dare take them off just yet.

He readjusted her in his arms so he could free up one of his hands. He wrapped one around her back, holding her in place, and used the other hand to tease her entrance.

He coated his fingers in her juices before sliding one of them inside her hot, tight pussy. Once it was inside her as far in as it would go, he twirled it around before pulling it back out to rub against the bundle of nerves.

Amberly broke the kiss on a moan as she leaned her head back in pleasure. Dain took the opportunity to trail kisses down her neck and chest, but her breasts were just out of reach.

When he pushed his finger back inside her, he lifted her up at the same time, bringing her breasts within his reach. He didn't hang around. Quickly sucking one hard nipple into his mouth, he flicked his tongue over the turgid tip.

Amberly grabbed his hair, holding his head against her chest. He could feel her heart pounding and knew his was beating just as fast.

He paid both breasts the same amount of attention as he pumped his finger in and out of her tight, wet pussy. Building up speed with each pass. As soon as he felt her walls tighten around his finger, he added another, sending her straight over the edge.

Her moans were music to his ears, but it wasn't what he was after. He wanted to hear her scream his name, and he would by the time he was finished with her.

When he felt her orgasm begin to ebb, he added a third finger, sending her over the edge again and prolonging the pleasure. Only when she was completely done did he remove his fingers.

He was too far gone to bother kicking off his shoe. He just undid his trousers as quickly as he could and pushed them down, releasing his swollen cock.

Without losing a beat, he lined up his cock with her entrance and pushed just the tip inside her.

Amberly gasped at the feel of him stretching her entrance, but she didn't stop him. Not that he would have been able to stop. He was way past that point. As soon as her hot moist pussy covered the tip of his cock, he was gone.

Who was he kidding? As soon as she stepped out of the river, water trailing down her naked body, he was gone. Maybe even before that.

He grabbed her by the back of the head and smashed his mouth against hers as he slowly pushed his cock the rest of the way in.

It took all of his willpower to enter her slowly, but he needed to give her the chance to adjust to his size. It would only cause her pain if he slammed straight in, and that was the last thing he wanted to do.

She had already suffered enough pain at the hands of the Vampires. He would not treat her the same way. It was either pleasure or nothing, and since he wasn't willing to settle for nothing, it would be pleasure.

Once he was fully seated, he held still for as long as he could, which wasn't easy. Her hot, moist pussy squeezed his cock tightly, threatening to steal the last of his control.

His cock pulsed inside her when she moaned into his mouth as their tongues franticly duelled one another. Dain couldn't get enough of her. He wanted... needed... more of her.

Even though he told himself to take it easy, he couldn't. He'd never felt as uncontrollable with a female in all his life. But with Amberly, it was like he didn't have any at all.

He broke the kiss as the last shreds of his control snapped. He couldn't stop from slamming into her over and over again, as hard as he could.

Whatever spell she had him under, at that moment in time, he didn't want it to stop.

Before he knew what he was doing, he had Amberly on all fours as he entered her from behind. Thankfully, even in his addled brain, he made sure she was kneeling on grass and not rocks.

As much as he enjoyed holding her in his arms, he was limited to how hard and fast he could go. But not in the new position. With her on all fours in front of him, he could fuck her harder and faster. Not to mention, deeper.

No matter how hard he slammed into her, she took all of him. Rocking in time with him, she held her position.

Dain could feel her walls tightening around his cock as she climbed closer to the edge.

He wasn't ready for it to be over with yet, but she didn't give him any choice. The second she tipped over the edge, she dragged him with her.

The urge to mate with her was incredibly strong. Stronger than he ever thought possible. Especially since he couldn't mate with a Human. Fuck them, yes. But he could only mate with one of his kind.

So, it took him by surprise when his fangs lengthened in his mouth, ready to mark her as his. It took every last ounce of willpower not to sink his fangs into her neck, tying her life to his for all eternity.

Instead, he bit his bottom lip. The coppery taste of his own blood filled his mouth, bring him back down to earth with a thud.

Amberly collapsed to the floor, her arms and legs giving out from under her. Dain rolled to the side, so he didn't squash her under his weight, and pulled her into his arms.

The second his cock slid free, he wanted to bury it inside her again. But until he could figure out why he had such a strong urge to mate with her, he couldn't risk it.

Her head rested on his chest as they both caught their breath. With his free hand, he gently brushed the hair out of her face.

"Are you okay?" he asked. "I didn't hurt you, did I?"

After she'd given him such pleasure, he would hate himself if he'd hurt her in any way. Just because she climaxed, it didn't mean he couldn't have hurt her in the process.

"Um… yeah, I'm okay," she said. "And you definitely didn't hurt me. Far from it."

"Good," he said.

Amberly smiled at him, and for a moment, he could've sworn he'd glimpsed amber in her blue eyes before she quickly blinked it away.

He knew some Humans had amber eyes, or flecks of amber, but theirs didn't glow. Only Shapeshifters had amber eyes that glowed. So why did hers? Or had he just imagined it?

Dain didn't have a clue, but he was determined to find out.

There were a lot of questions surrounding Amberly, he just hoped he could figure out the answers to some of them before he did something stupid. Like mating with her.

Chapter 13

What the fuck have I just done?

Never in her life had she been so bold, and definitely not with a monster. No matter what type he was, he was still a monster.

A sexy Shapeshifter! Her mind threw at her.

Yes, he was sexy, but it still didn't excuse the fact he'd hunted down and killed her kind nearly to extinction.

She knew he wasn't the only one. Others had played a part in bring her kind to extinction as well, but she wasn't sure she could look past his part in it.

Obviously some part of me can, otherwise I wouldn't have just thrown myself at him!

She not only let him pleasure her, but she'd encouraged him. All but throwing herself at him.

Amberly didn't have a clue what the hell had come

over her. It was like an unseen force pulling her towards him. Even if she'd wanted to stop, she didn't think she would have been able to.

There were no words to describe how embarrassed she was. How the hell was she supposed to look him in the eye? Especially when they were back with Natalia and Taredd?

She didn't know how she was going to pretend that nothing had happened between them when her mind was going to constantly remind her. They hadn't even left the river yet, and her mind had replayed it several times already.

She wished she could hide away at the river, at least until she could figure out what to do, but she knew that wasn't possible. Sooner or later, they needed to return to their campsite and Natalia. She'd already been gone long enough.

No doubt Natalia would have questions for her when she returned. For starters, she'd want to know what took her so long. What was she supposed to say? *'Sorry, I was busy fucking the Shapeshifter'*?

Yeah, she didn't think that would go down too well. Or maybe it would? After all, there was something going on between Natalia and Taredd. So, maybe Natalia wouldn't have a problem with it.

Even if Natalia didn't have a problem with it, Amberly did. At least, she should have, but deep down, she didn't.

Curled up in his arms listening to his heart beating, Amberly felt safe, protected... wanted. She didn't want to leave the warmth of his arms.

As much as she didn't like to admit the truth out loud sometimes, she refused to lie to herself. She had spent so many years lying to the people around her, she didn't want to lie to herself as well.

"We'll have to get back soon," Dain said, finally breaking the silence.

He tickled her arm with his fingers, relaxing her even more. She could quite happily fall asleep, she was so content in that moment.

"I know," she said on a sigh.

She was hoping they had more time, but she knew he was right. There was only so long she could be away from Natalia before she came looking for her. She was surprised she hadn't already.

Oh god! What if she has?

What if she'd seen them together? Amberly definitely wouldn't be able to look any of them in the eye then.

"We have enough time to clean off in the river first," he told her, unaware of her internal struggle.

Amberly hadn't even thought about that. She'd been so lost in her thoughts, it hadn't even entered her mind to clean up in the river before going back to camp.

It was bad enough knowing Taredd had more than likely heard them, but she certainly didn't want to confirm what they did by walking around smelling of Dain.

She didn't know much about Taredd and his species of Demon, or any Demon for that matter. But she knew a lot about Dain's species, like how strong their sense of smell was.

Her mother had made sure she knew more about Dain's kind than any of the others. She would say it was because they were even more deadly than the others. Amberly wasn't so sure her mother had been right.

After everything she'd seen, Shapeshifters were far from the most deadly. She reserved that title for the Vampires.

"Thanks," she said as she sat up. "I'll do that now."

"I think I'll join you," he said, sitting up next to her.

She wasn't so sure that was a good idea. What if she jumped on him again? They definitely didn't have time for round two.

She didn't know if she could trust herself alone with him while they were both fully dressed, let alone being completely naked in the river together. It was already evident that she couldn't keep her hands off him.

She couldn't exactly say no to him joining her, though. She just hoped she could control herself.

Dain took off the last of his clothing, then stood up and held out his hand for her. He effortlessly pulled her to her feet and steadied her when she wobbled slightly.

Amberly was surprised at how comfortable she felt around him, even though she was naked. She had noticed when he'd cleaned her wounds that she didn't feel uncomfortable.

She had brushed it off at the time, thinking it was because of everything she'd been through. But now, she wasn't so sure that was the reason after all.

Something about him made her feel like she could do anything, be anything. Like she could take on the world.

Her mouth went dry as she took in her first full look of his incredible body. The man was huge, and not just his height. He towered over her.

His arms were thicker than her thighs, yet she didn't feel the slightest bit intimidated by him. And his chest? Well, she could easily hide behind him and nobody would be able to see her.

She already knew how strong he was, from when he'd carried her away from the Vampires, and again when he'd lifted her into his arms. But it was nothing compared to seeing his muscular body with her own eyes.

No wonder he could hold me easily.

She mentally kicked herself for not spending more time memorising the feel of his muscles underneath her fingertips when she had the chance. She itched to run her hands over his washboard abs, and follow the dusky trail of hair down to his still rock-hard cock.

Surely that beast should have started to go down by now?

The men she'd been with in the past had been well and truly soft by now.

She was tempted to climb back up him and impale herself again, but somehow, she held herself back.

Yay! Go me!

Dragging her eyes away from him, she headed back into the river. She didn't want to wet her hair any more than it already was, so she tied it in a knot on top of her head.

It was getting late, and she didn't want to freeze to death because her hair didn't have time to dry. As it was, she'd left it later than she should have, but she had no choice.

She would have waited until morning, but she needed to wash the dirt and grime from her hair and her body. She could still smell the stench of Vampires all over her and it made her physically sick.

A moment later, water splashed behind her as Dain joined her in the river. He handed her the bar of soap she'd dropped earlier.

They washed in silence before returning to the shore.

"Here," he said, handing her the towel when she went to pick up the clean t-shirt. "Dry off first before putting your clothes on. You don't want to sit outside in wet clothes at night, even with the fire."

She had completely forgotten that Natalia had given her a towel with the clean clothes. She had left it at the top of the pile, but it must have been knocked off when they had been busy.

Which made sense because none of the clothes were in a neat pile anymore. Both clean and dirty were scattered about.

"Thank you," she said, taking the towel from him.

Keeping her eyes averted as best she could, she quickly dried off before passing it back. She nearly tipped over when she pulled on the trousers, but she was able to catch her balance at the last second.

The last thing she wanted to do was face-plant the floor with her trousers around her ankles.

By the time she finished pulling on the t-shirt, Dain was fully dressed and waiting for her.

She slipped her feet into the shoes and picked up the pile of dirty clothes then turned to him.

"Ready?" he asked.

"Um… yes, I think so," she said, double checking the floor for anything she might have missed.

"Good," Dain said. "Dinner shouldn't be too long."

"Thank god," she said. "I'm starving."

Her stomach chose that moment to rumble.

"I can tell," he said, smiling at her. "Come on, let's get back. We don't want Natalia sending out another search party for you."

She didn't say a word as she followed him back through the woods.

Amberly thought that was why Dain was there. Natalia had sent him to check up on her. She probably didn't believe Amberly wouldn't run off at the first chance she got.

Thankfully, Natalia hadn't come looking for her as well, otherwise she'd have a lot of explaining to do. Not that she owned anyone an explanation, least of all Natalia.

She seemed to have her own thing going on with Taredd. So, she had no room to talk when it came to fraternising with the enemy.

The more time she was around those two, the more she was convinced something was going on between them. She was dying to ask Natalia, but they hadn't been alone and she didn't want Taredd and Dain overhearing their conversation, even if it involved one of them.

She would have brought it up when they walked to

the river together earlier, but they hadn't really been on their own. If Amberly could hear the river from where they'd stopped to make camp, then there was no doubt in her mind that Dain and Taredd could as well. Which meant they would have heard their entire conversation.

Sometimes Amberly wished her hearing wasn't that good. Especially when she was locked in a bunker with a group of other people, but more so when she was held captive in the Vampire camp.

She always knew when the Vampires were coming to her tent, even if they hadn't said a word. She could tell when their footsteps were getting closer.

Images flashed through her mind, and not the good kind. Hands grabbing, pain as razor-sharp teeth pierced shin, and blood. Lots of blood, all around her.

Amberly took two more steps and then bent over to heave behind a bush. No matter how much she heaved, nothing but bile came up because she had nothing in her stomach.

"Are you okay?" Concern laced Dain's voice as he raced over to her and placed a comforting hand on her back.

"Yeah, I'm good," she said.

The sound of Dain's voice, along with his touch, chased the demons from her mind and she was able to stand upright again. He helped steady her when her legs tried to give out under her.

"Sorry," she said as she looked up at him. "I don't know what came over me, but I'm good now."

The concern on his face spread warmth through her,

136

chasing away the last remnants of nausea. Not to mention the feel of his strong arms holding her tight against him.

"Are you sure?" he asked.

"Yeah, I'm fine," she said. "I promise."

"Okay," he said, not sounding as if he believed her. "If there is something wrong, you can tell me though. I won't say anything to Natalia or Taredd."

"You wouldn't need to say anything to Taredd. He can hear us." The words slipped out of her mouth before she could think better of it.

Taredd had already heard more than what she was comfortable with, so she wasn't bothered about him hearing what she was saying now. As it was, she didn't know how she was going to look him in the eye after he heard everything she'd done with Dain at the river.

She didn't have a single doubt in her mind that he heard everything they had done. It was probably the reason why Natalia hadn't come looking for them. She probably knew about it as well.

Oh, god!

Amberly should have known better, and she would have done in any other situation, but she hadn't been able to control herself. It was like somebody else had taken over her body and she was just there for the ride.

But what a ride it had been!

Amberly knew it was wrong to sleep with the enemy, but that didn't stop her from wanting to climb up him and do it all over again. Yep, she was well and truly fucked in the head.

How could she possibly want to have sex with a monster? Because the monster was Dain, that's why. If it was anybody else, she would have been able to stay well away.

"That's true," he said after a moment. "He can hear us. But I promise, he won't say anything to Natalia if you don't want her to know."

"Honestly, there's nothing wrong," she told him.

She certainly wasn't about to confess all to him. She didn't even know him.

That didn't stop you from fucking him though! Her mind threw at her. *Yeah, but who wouldn't?* She answered back.

She mentally shook her head. It wasn't the first time she'd argued with herself, and it wouldn't be the last.

Dain scrutinized her for a moment and then nodded his head. "Okay, just know that you can tell me anything, anytime. If you want to keep it between the two of us, I can make sure Taredd is out of hearing range."

"Thanks," she said.

It was nice of him to offer, but it was unlikely she would take him up on it.

They walked in silence the rest of the way back to camp. Natalia and Taredd were sat by a small fire eating dinner by the time they arrived.

Amberly noticed the horse and cart had been moved a lot closer to the fire than they were last time they stopped. Taredd hadn't hooked the horse up to the cart again either.

She wondered if they were stopping for longer, or if

they were just giving the horse more of a rest.

The large animal stood to one side with a bag covering its mouth. She could see its jaw moving as it grazed on whatever was inside.

Even though it was no longer attached to the cart, it was still tied up, unable to escape. It still had the straps around its head, but the rest had been removed.

Amberly knew how the poor animal must feel. Even though she'd been freed from the Vampires, she still wasn't free to leave if she wanted to. She had given her word to Natalia that she wouldn't leave, so she wouldn't.

The fire licked at the bottom of a large metal pot. It hung suspended above the flames by three long poles.

She didn't need to look inside the pot to know there was food cooking away inside. It smelt so good that Amberly's stomach rumbled loud enough for everyone to hear.

"Did you enjoy your swim?" Natalia asked as Amberly sat opposite her.

"Um… yes, I did," she said.

She could feel her cheeks heating at the memory of how much she enjoyed her time at the river, and it had absolutely nothing to do with swimming. No, it was all down to Dain.

Amberly still didn't have a clue what came over her. But one thing was for sure, she didn't regret it one bit.

Nope, definitely don't feel regret. Embarrassment is way up there, though.

"You must be starving now," Natalia said.

Amberly thought her stomach growling would have given that away, but it just proved her point about Natalia's hearing not being very good.

"Absolutely starving," Amberly said.

"Don't worry," Natalia said. "There's plenty of food."

While she'd been speaking with Natalia, Dain had grabbed two bowls from the cart and filled them with the food that was cooking over the fire. He handed one to her before taking a seat right next to her.

Forget the heat from the fire. The heat coming from Dain was more than enough to set her ablaze.

"We've been talking while you two have been gone," Taredd said to Dain. "And we've decided to stop here for the night."

"Do you think that's a wise idea?" Dain asked. "It wouldn't take much for the Vampires to catch up, especially after nightfall."

"Yes, I know," Taredd said. "But we're all exhausted. We need to rest for at least a couple of hours."

Amberly could see both their points. She was beyond exhausted and could do with some sleep. But on the other hand, she did not want to be caught by the Vampires again. Her last stay with them was more than enough for one lifetime.

"Okay," Dain said. "We'll stop, but only for a couple of hours. I don't like being out in the open like this."

"We can always find a tavern to stop at next time," Taredd said. "Then we won't be out in the open like this."

"No, we'll be backed into a corner instead," Dain

said. "Look how it ended the last time you stopped at a tavern."

"That's not going to happen again," Taredd said adamantly.

Amberly didn't have a clue what they were going on about, but whatever it was, Dain wasn't happy about it.

"Fine," he finally relented. "We'll stop at the next tavern we come across."

"Good," Taredd said. "But we're still stopping here for a while now. We all need a rest, the horse included."

She had to admit, she could do with a break from the cart.

Chapter 14

Dain didn't like the idea of stopping at a tavern one bit. Not after everything that happened with Natalia and the Demons.

He was surprised Taredd even suggested staying in another one, but he couldn't blame him. It would be a lot more comfortable than sleeping on the ground out in the open.

As much as Dain enjoyed sleeping under the stars, he would much prefer to be lying on a nice soft mattress. Back home, he would often be found sleeping under the stars on a daybed by the pool.

Too many years had passed since he was last home. He'd forgotten what it was like sleeping in his own bed. Maybe now that they were no longer hunting down Humans, he could return to his home. It would be great to see his family again.

"If you don't mind me asking, what happened last time you stayed in a tavern?" Amberly asked.

Taredd and Dain shared a look. Neither of them wanted to scare her, but it would be better if she knew what happened. That way, she would be less likely to do something stupid, like run off.

"Um…" Natalia began. "Well, you see…"

"What Natalia is trying to say, is we stopped overnight in a tavern," Taredd filled in for Natalia. "Everything was going fine until I went for a walk the next morning."

"Yep, it was really nice until then," Natalia added. "I've never slept in a bed so comfy in all my life. It was a dream."

"What happened the next morning?" Amberly asked.

"When I woke up, Taredd was already gone," Natalia told her. "I was just about to get up when somebody knocked on the door. Before I had a chance to move, the door was kicked in and two Demons came rushing in. I tried screaming for help, but one of them punched me in the face, knocking me out cold."

"Shit!" Amberly said. "What happened next?"

"When I woke up, I was in a different building with the two Demons who had taken me and they had a friend with them. Thankfully, Taredd and Dain came to my rescue."

"Unfortunately, it wasn't in time to stop them from harming you," Taredd said, looking down at Natalia with guilt in his eyes.

"But you stopped them from doing something worse,"

Natalia told him.

Dain could see Amberly was trying to figure out what was going on between Taredd and Natalia. She hadn't asked outright, but he knew she wanted to. Why she hadn't already was a mystery to him. He thought they were supposed to be best friends, didn't that mean they could speak freely between them?

Maybe she was waiting to be alone with Natalia, where neither he nor Taredd could overhear them, but that would not happen. He knew Taredd certainly wouldn't be happy if they wondered out of earshot.

"Don't look so worried," Natalia said to Amberly when she finally dragged her eyes off Taredd. "These two will keep us safe."

"Sounds like it," Amberly mumbled quietly.

Dain and Taredd shared a look. They both heard her, but by the looks of it, Natalia hadn't. She continued talking about what happened to her, giving Amberly every little detail.

"She's right," Dain whispered next to her. "We will keep you safe, I give you my word."

"We'll see," she barely breathed the words, but he still heard her.

It was like she was testing him, to see how good his hearing was.

Two can play that game.

"Yes, you will," he spoke just as quietly.

He wasn't expecting her to hear him, but to his surprise, she did.

"Anyway," Natalia continued. "Thanks to Dain's

wonder medicine, I'm completely healed."

"Good, I'm glad you're better," Amberly said.

"You'll be healed soon as well," Natalia said.

"I already am," she told her.

Dain hadn't been thinking straight when he'd seen her by the river, otherwise he would have realised at the time that she was no longer covered in cuts and bruises. Technically, he hadn't been thinking straight since he first set eyes on her, but that was beside the point.

He should have noticed, and would have done if she hadn't put him under some sort of spell. That was the only explanation he could come up with to why he couldn't think straight with her around.

He just hoped he could pull his shit together before they reached the next town.

"See?" Natalia said. "It's good stuff, isn't it? I was amazed at how fast my wounds healed. I don't know what he uses, but it's a hell of a lot better than anything we've made in the past."

"You've made your own medicine before?" Dain asked.

"Yes," Natalia said. "Well, we've attempted to, anyway. Sometimes it works, but most of the time it doesn't. Finding the ingredients for some of them is the hardest part."

"Well, I'm more than happy to teach you the methods I use," he offered. "I'll even show you where to find the ingredients."

"That would be fantastic," Natalia said. "Thank you."

"Yes, thank you," Amberly added. "It's very kind of

you."

"You're more than welcome," he told them.

Amberly placed the empty bowl on the floor next to her and then covered a yawn with the back of her hand. A second later, Natalia followed suit.

"Excuse me," she said when she'd finished. "I'm shattered."

"Me too," Natalia said.

"We could all do with some sleep," Taredd said. "We've got a long journey ahead of us."

"I'll take first watch," Dain said.

There were too many dangers around to let their guard down. So, one of them needed to keep watch while the rest slept. He was more than happy to take the first watch. It would give him time to figure out what was going on between him and Amberly.

"We can sleep on the cart, Amberly," Natalia said. "There's plenty of space for the two of us, and more than enough blankets. Plus, it won't be bumpy this time."

"I'm good here on the floor," Amberly said. "But thanks anyway."

"Are you sure?" Natalia asked her.

"Yep, I'm sure," she said. "I'd rather stay by the fire, if that's okay."

"Of course it's okay," Taredd said. "Wherever you feel comfortable. But I must add, there is only one bedroll."

"That's okay," she said. "I'll be fine on the floor."

"If you insist," Taredd said.

Even if she was fine on the floor, Dain wasn't happy

about it. He should have picked up a couple of bedrolls, but he hadn't thought about that at the time. His only concern had been Natalia.

He was kicking himself now though, for not planning ahead. He knew they were looking for her friends, but he honestly didn't think any of them would still be alive.

"I packed more than enough blankets," Dain said. "I'm sure we could put a few on the floor for you to sleep on."

"Thank you," she said. "But honestly, I'll be fine on the floor."

Dain didn't care if she would be fine or not. He would not let her sleep rough on the floor. Not when he could do something about it.

It may not be much, but a few blankets laid out on the floor was better than nothing. If he could give her a soft bed to sleep on, he would. Even if it meant staying in another tavern.

As long as either he or Taredd stayed by the female's sides at all times, they shouldn't have a problem like before. He certainly would not leave Amberly by herself like Taredd had done with Natalia.

Taredd made a massive mistake leaving Natalia on her own in the bedroom which gave some other Demons the opportunity to snatch her. He was frantic by the time Dain had caught up with him. He even accused Dain of being the one to take her.

Luckily, Dain was able to track down the culprits, and they were able to get Natalia back. Unfortunately, it wasn't before the Demons had laid their hands on her.

Dain could still see some of the bruises they left on her, but it could have been a whole lot worse if they hadn't acted quickly. If Taredd hadn't returned to their room, if Dain hadn't spotted him and followed him inside, it could have ended badly for Natalia.

"Can we get another bedroll from the next town we stop at?" Natalia asked.

Dain had already decided he was going to pick up another one for Amberly, but there was no telling when that would be. It could turn out to be quicker to go back to the last town they stopped at, but he didn't think that would be a wise idea. For one thing, it was too close to the Vampires camp.

"Yes, we'll get another one as soon as we can," Taredd said. "We'll stock up with more supplies at the next town and pick up a couple of bedrolls. I don't know about Dain, but I'm fed up of sleeping on the hard floor as well."

"Oh, yes," Dain agreed. "I've more than had my fill of sleeping rough."

"Hopefully, we'll come across a town tomorrow," Taredd said.

"Don't you know where the next one is?" Natalia asked.

"No," Taredd shook his head. "To be honest, it's the first time we've been this side of the mountain."

"Us too," Natalia said.

That surprised Dain. He knew Humans moved around a lot, so he just assumed they'd been there before.

It was obvious some Humans had been, otherwise

there wouldn't have been any towns in the area. But he hadn't realised it was the first time Natalia and Amberly had been there.

"How long have you been here?" Taredd asked her.

"I arrived just before you came across me," she told him. "Amberly arrived with the others a couple of days ahead of me."

"You arrived the same time as us then," Taredd told her. "Because it wasn't long after I got here that I spotted you."

Dain couldn't help but feel sorry for them. After everything they'd been through in their lives, to then be grabbed just as they found a new area. Yeah, he felt sorry for them.

"It wasn't long after we arrived that Bella showed up with the Vampires," Amberly said. "So, we hadn't been here long either."

Sadness filled her voice as she spoke. The urge to pull her into his arms and tell her that everything was going to be okay was strong.

It wasn't the first time he'd wanted to comfort a female, but it was the first time the urge to comfort had been so powerful, it was difficult to hold himself back.

He wasn't sure she'd welcome his touch after what they did by the river. But more than that, he didn't trust himself to touch her again. Not after losing control of himself earlier.

"I wish they hadn't killed that bitch," Natalia said angrily. "I would love to have been the one to end her for what she's done."

"Trust me," Amberly said. "She got what she deserved, and then some."

Dain could imagine she did, and he bet Amberly was made to watch every second of it.

"Anyway, I am really tired," Amberly said. "If you don't mind, I don't want to think about it anymore, I just want to get some sleep."

"Yes, of course," Natalia said.

"I'll get the blankets for you," Dain said.

He picked up her empty bowl along with his and carried them back to the cart. They could wait until the morning to be washed.

He grabbed a pile of blankets from the back of the cart and then returned to the fire. He cleared the ground from sticks and stones as best he could before laying out the blankets.

"It's not great," he said when he was done. "But it's better than nothing."

"It's perfect, thank you," she said.

"Well, I'll see you in the morning," Natalia said. "If you change your mind about sleeping on the cart, you're more than welcome to join me."

"I'm good," Amberly said again. "But thanks for the offer."

Natalia stopped next to Amberly on her way to the cart. Before Amberly could react, Natalia gave her a quick hug.

"It really is good to see you," Natalia said.

"You too," Amberly said, giving her a small smile in return. "I'll see you in the morning."

"Yes, see you in the morning."

Neither female spoke another word as they both got ready for bed.

"Sweet dreams, my love," Taredd whispered to Natalia as he tucked a blanket around her.

"You too," she replied sleepily.

A moment later, Taredd re-joined him by the fire. They sat in silence for a while, waiting for Amberly and Natalia to drift off to sleep. It took a while, but eventually, both of their breathing evened out.

"So," Taredd whispered. "I heard what happened by the river."

"I thought you did," Dain said.

"I take it she doesn't want Natalia to know?"

"I have no idea what she wants," Dain said. "And I'm not stupid enough to try guessing. If she decides to tell Natalia, then that's her choice. I won't be the one saying anything, and neither should you."

"You know I would never say anything," Taredd said. "It's not my place."

Yes, Dain knew that. Which was why they were both speaking low enough that neither female should be able to overhear them, even if they were awake.

But Amberly's different, his mind reminded him.

She was different. Between the glimpse of glowing amber he'd noticed in her eyes, and her being able to hear the river when Natalia couldn't, he was beginning to think she wasn't completely Human. But if she wasn't Human, then what was she?

He would have thought she was a Shapeshifter like

him, but if she was, her eyes would glow all the time. That was the one thing they couldn't change, no matter what they shifted into. Their eyes always gave them away.

"I don't think it's wise to stay too long," Dain said, changing the subject.

He really didn't want to talk about what was going on between him and Amberly, especially since he didn't have a clue what had happened, far less what they were going to do about it.

"I know," Taredd said. "But they needed sleep, and they weren't getting any in the back of the cart while it was moving. They're not like us, they can't stay awake for days on end."

"Yes, I know," Dain said. "That still doesn't change the fact that we can't stay too long. We still don't know why the Vampires kept Amberly alive. Until we do, we have to assume they still want her. And therefore, are coming after her."

"So, you didn't find out anything while you were alone with her?" Taredd asked.

"No," he lied.

Until he knew for sure she wasn't completely Human, he didn't want to say anything to Taredd. Plus, he had a feeling she could hear their conversation no matter how quietly they spoke.

He wasn't convinced she was really asleep either. He had a feeling she was pretending to sleep. No doubt waiting for them to drift off before she made a run for it. Not that she had anywhere to go.

No, it definitely wasn't safe for her on her own, especially if he was right about the Vampires.

Chapter 15

Three days had passed since she was rescued from the Vampires. They had covered quite some distance from the Vampires camp in that time, but they hadn't seen any sign of Dain and Taredd's friend or a town.

In fact, they hadn't seen any sign of life other than the local wildlife. Amberly enjoyed listening to the birds singing in the trees, but she was beginning to hate the horse and cart. More so the cart than the horse.

Her arse hurt from the bumpy ride. She was tempted to jump out and walk, but she knew Dain and Taredd wouldn't be happy with her doing that. It would slow them down.

She understood why they were in such a hurry. She heard them speaking at night about it when they thought she was asleep. They thought the Vampires kept her alive for a reason, and that they would come after her because of that reason.

The only problem was, neither of them knew why. Amberly would tell them if she knew, but she was just as in the dark about it as they were.

So, all day, every day, they travelled. Stopping occasionally in the daytime, but only long enough so they could all relieve themselves, or eat. Then they would be straight back on the road.

Thankfully, as soon as night fell, they would stop and make camp for the night. She didn't think she could cope if they decided to travel through the night as well.

It was nice camping out under the stars. It would be better if she had something more than blankets to sleep on, but it was better than sleeping next to Natalia on the cart. She'd rather sleep on the cold, hard ground than spend a second more on the cart.

Since her moment of madness at the river with Dain, Amberly had managed to control herself. Mostly because she refused to be left alone with him.

Wherever Natalia went, so did she. She knew Natalia wanted to spend some time by herself with Taredd. Could see it in her eyes whenever she looked at him. But Amberly didn't trust herself around Dain.

She still didn't know what came over her the last time they were alone, and she didn't want a repeat.

Well, technically, you do, her mind threw at her. *Shut up!*

Amberly couldn't keep count of the amount of times she'd replayed their time together in her mind. No matter what she tried, it was on constantly replay.

It didn't help that the guy was a walking sex god. Every time she looked at him, she could feel her blood heating up. He was dangerous, and it had absolutely nothing to do with him being a Shapeshifter. Though that played a pretty big part.

All the while she was having an internal conflict over Dain, Natalia was excited she was still with them. She talked non-stop about their future in the Demon realm, living in Taredd's home.

That was certainly one place she didn't want to live out the rest of her life. It was one thing hanging around them in the Human realm because she knew what to expect. But the Demon realm? She would rather not go there, let alone live there.

It didn't matter how much he tried to reassure her it would be safe, she didn't want to go there.

If it came down to a choice between the Demons and the Shapeshifters, Amberly wasn't sure she could choose. Part of her wanted to stay with Natalia and go wherever she went. But a bigger part of her wanted to stay with Dain.

"What you thinking about?" Natalia asked, snapping her out of her thoughts.

"Nothing," she lied. "I was just listening to the birds."

She couldn't exactly say she was fantasizing about Dain.

"It is lovely listening to them, isn't it?" Natalia said.

"Yes, it is," she agreed, which wasn't a lie.

She did enjoy listening to them and watching them

flying around. She could watch them for hours.

She hadn't been able to enjoy them in the past. It was too dangerous to stop and enjoy them in the day, and they were never around when she snuck out of the bunker at night. But the stars, they were always there to greet her.

"You would love it in my realm," Dain said. "They sing all day and night there."

"Really?" she and Natalia asked in unison.

"Yep," he said.

"Don't they keep you awake?" Natalia asked.

"No," he laughed. "Only if you leave the windows open."

Amberly bet it was nice to open a window and listen to the birds without having to go outside. Bunkers didn't have windows. Well, none she'd stayed in anyway.

She knew about them and how they worked from many of the old rundown buildings she'd scavenged from in the past. Most of the glass had been broken, but the mechanics were still there, and some even worked. They weren't much different to how the bunker doors operated.

"Is it the same in your realm?" Natalia asked Taredd.

"Unfortunately, not," he said. "There are birds in my realm, but they don't sound as nice as the ones here or in other realms, like Dain's."

"That's a shame," she said. "It would be nice to listen to them at night."

"I'm sure we can visit Dain's home," he told her. "But first, let's concentrate on finding Arun and making it back to mine."

"That would be wonderful," she bounced. "Wouldn't it Amberly?"

Amberly nodded her head. If she was being honest though, she would much rather stay in Dain's realm. It seemed to be the best option out of the two so far.

"Who is Arun?" Amberly asked.

They had mentioned the name a few times, but she was still none the wiser to who, or what, he was. She knew he was male by the way they spoke about him, but that is all she knew.

"He's our friend," Taredd told her. "He usually travels with us, but we split up not long after we reached this side of the mountain."

"He is a Fae," Dain said before she had the chance to ask.

"Oh," she said in surprise.

She didn't know much about the Fae, other than they were magical creatures.

"Is Arun's realm like either of yours?" Natalia asked.

"More like Dain's than mine," Taredd said.

"But more fancy," Dain said. "They like everything to be pristine all the time."

"Yes, they do like everything to gleam," Taredd said.

"I bet they love you two visiting." As soon as the words left her month, Amberly wished she could take them back.

She didn't mean it in a bad way, but she knew that's how it must have sounded.

Instead of taking offence, however, they both burst

out laughing.

"We do stand out whenever we visit," Taredd laughed. "I suppose it doesn't help that I always wear black clothing."

Amberly was thinking more along the lines of their dirty clothes from sleeping on the ground, but she would not correct him.

"I think she means how dirty we are," Dain said. "But yes, Amberly, they don't like us visiting, and will look down their noses at us."

"Not to mention, they see us as lesser beings," Taredd said.

"But Arun doesn't," she said.

She didn't know if that was true or not, but she had a feeling she was right.

"No, Arun doesn't see us that way," Dain said. "The three of us may be different species, but we are all equal, and so are you."

It was nice of him to say, but she knew it wasn't true. Humans were at the bottom of the food chain, and she knew that. It didn't mean she had to like it, though.

"Hopefully, you'll get to meet him soon enough," Taredd said. "And then you can see for yourself what he's like."

That's what she was dreading. Meeting Arun. Dain and Taredd had been really nice to her and Natalia so far, but that didn't mean things weren't going to change once they caught up with Arun.

It could all be a rouse for all her or Natalia knew. They could be keeping them sweet so they would go along quietly, but they could ultimately be planning on selling them to the highest bidder.

Amberly really hoped not. She didn't like her chances of escaping if that were the case.

"At this moment in time," Natalia said, changing the subject. "I would just be happy for a nice hot bath and a soft bed."

"You and me both," Dain said. "I'm getting too old for sleeping on the floor."

"What do you mean getting?" Taredd laughed.

"You've got no room to talk," Dain said. "You're older than me."

Amberly knew she was going to regret asking, but she couldn't help herself. "How old are you both?"

"How old do you think we are?" Dain asked as he spun around in his seat to look at her.

"I don't know," she said.

"Guess," he told her. "It doesn't matter what you say, you won't offend me."

"Okay," she said. "You look around thirty years."

Dain smiled as he said. "Add another zero on the end, and you'll be close."

Amberly's mouth dropped open.

Three hundred years old! Oh, my god!

"See?" Taredd said. "He's an old bastard."

"But still not as old as you," Dain pointed out. "I'm three hundred and fifty-two years old, and Taredd is three hundred and seventy-five."

"So, we're like babies compared to you," Natalia said. "I'm only twenty-five."

"Not babies, no," Taredd said. "But yes, you are a lot younger than us."

"I would say so," Amberly blurted.

She really needed to think before she spoke. One of these days, her mouth was going to get her in trouble. Thankfully, today wasn't that day. Both Taredd and Dain laughed.

Amberly couldn't help but wonder how that was going to work for Natalia and Taredd's relationship. Natalia would eventually grow old and die, like the rest of their kind, but Taredd would live on. Possibly for hundreds of years.

She could see Natalia was thinking the same thing. Sadness filled her eyes.

She wanted to comfort her friend, but she didn't know how, or if it was even possible. If Natalia truly loved Taredd, which Amberly was starting to think was the case, then it was bound to be breaking her heart at the thought of him living on without her.

Unfortunately, there was no other way around it.

Her own heart hurt with the knowledge. She wanted to tell herself it was for Natalia, but it would be a lie. It was her own heartache, and it was all for Dain.

As much as she tried to fight it, she couldn't stop herself for falling for the Shapeshifter. She knew it was stupid, but there it was. Not only was he the sexiest man she'd ever seen, but he was also kind and caring.

The thought of only having a few precious years with him hurt her heart more than she ever thought possible.

She couldn't look at Natalia without seeing the heartache she felt reflexed back at her. As she looked away from Natalia, her eyes clashed with Dain's. She realised then that he'd been watching her the entire time she'd been looking at Natalia.

She hoped she hadn't given away her own feelings by letting her guard down and showing it on her face, but she probably had. Normally, she was pretty good at hiding her feelings. Yes, she had trouble controlling her mouth at times, but she was good at controlling her facial expression. Except for when it came to Dain.

No matter what she tried, she couldn't hide her feeling from him. He seemed to be able to see right through her. But that didn't mean she was willing to admit how she felt. At least, not out loud.

Thankfully, he didn't say anything. He just smiled warmly before turning back around. That small smile was enough to set butterflies off in her stomach.

Stupid or not, Amberly was falling deeper and deeper in love with a Shapeshifter. With Dain.

Chapter 16

It was good that Amberly was asking questions about him and Taredd. It was a vast improvement from when they rescued her.

He'd noticed over the last couple of days she enjoyed listening to the birds. But it didn't stop with just the birds. She seemed to love anything to do with nature.

She perked up when he told her about the birds in his realm singing all day and night. He would love to show her his realm, he knew she would appreciate its beauty.

It surprised him how well she and Natalia had taken the news about how old he and Taredd were. He knew it was a shock to hear they were over three hundred years older than either of them.

The age difference didn't bother him. Being immortal, age became nothing more than a number. But to a

Human who was mortal, it might be a problem.

After all, they would grow old and eventually die while an immortal would look the same, no matter how old they got.

He could tell by the look on Natalia's face when she looked at Taredd that she wasn't bothered by the age difference. He just hoped it wasn't a problem for Amberly either. If it was, he would try to convince her the age gap wasn't an issue, but other than that, there wasn't much he could do about it.

He couldn't change the fact he was much older than her. He could only try to change how she felt about it.

He'd kept his promise over the last couple of days to teach them about herbal medicine. Natalia wasn't as interested as Amberly. She always got bored after a few minutes, but Amberly listened intently as he explained all the benefits of the herbs they came across on their journey.

Whenever they stopped, he would point out different plants and tell her all about them. Which ones could be used in medicine, and more importantly, which ones to stay well away from.

The last thing he wanted was for either of them to accidentally poison themselves. Not that Natalia paid much attention to any of it.

He had to admit, he wasn't all that bothered about Natalia not wanting to learn. She wasn't his concern. Amberly, however, was a completely different matter.

As far as he was concerned, she was his to protect. And that meant teaching her everything he knew. If he thought it would do any good, he would teach her to fight as well, but he knew that would be a waste of time since all of her opponents had an unfair advantage.

"I think we're close," Taredd said, breaking into Dain's thoughts.

"Good," Dain said. "I'm starving."

"When aren't you?" Taredd asked.

Dain didn't bother replying to Taredd's comment. Instead, he added, "And I'm looking forward to a nice hot bath."

"I thought you would have wanted a nice cold beer," Taredd said.

"Yeah, that too," Dain agreed.

"Well, they all sound good to me," Taredd said.

"Me too," Natalia said. "But add in a nice warm bed as well."

Dain laughed. "That's a given."

"Don't worry, my love," Taredd said, smiling. "There will definitely be a nice warm bed for you."

"Thank God for that," she said. "Not that I don't like this way of travelling, but I've had enough of sleeping on the cart. The bedroll helps, but it's still not very comfortable."

"No, it's not," Taredd agreed.

"It's not been too bad on the blankets on the floor," Amberly said. "I've had no trouble sleeping."

Dain knew for a fact Amberly hadn't slept as well as she was making out. She would lie awake for hours, pretending to be asleep. Then when she finally drifted off, she would toss and turn the entire time.

Something was keeping her awake, and he had a feeling he knew exactly what it was.

"Is that it? Is that where we're going?" Natalia asked as she pointed at a small scattering of building ahead of them.

The small village was nestled amongst the trees, hiding it from view until they were nearly upon it. Dain guessed there couldn't be more than a hundred people living there. But he wasn't complaining, it made his job easier in keeping Amberly safe. The fewer people around, the less likely any of them would start something.

"Yes, that's where we're going," Taredd said. "But don't worry, nobody will bother you this time, I'll make sure of it."

"I'm not worried," she said, looking all gooey eyed at him. "I know you'll come for me again."

"You can always count on that," he said, looking just as gooey eyed at her.

"Get a room," Dain said, rolling his eyes.

"We will be soon," Taredd said, smirking at Dain.

Taredd and Natalia were eager to be alone. They hadn't been able to spend any time alone over the last couple of days. Every time they tried, they failed. It didn't matter where they said they were going, or what they were doing, Amberly would ask to go with them.

They were both too polite to tell her what they really wanted to do, so they would make up excuses. Dain had a feeling if they just told her the true, she would leave them in peace.

He certainly wasn't going to point it out if they weren't. He was having too much fun watching Taredd suffer. He deserved it after all the times he'd cock-blocked Dain in the past.

He knew what Amberly was doing. She was avoiding being on her own with him, but unfortunately, that wasn't going to work when they reached the tavern.

There was no way Taredd and Natalia would want to share a room with her, and she certainly couldn't have her own room because it was too dangerous. He didn't want a repeat of what happened to Natalia.

So, she would have to share with him. Which meant she was going to be alone with him whether she liked it or not.

Dain wouldn't force her to do something she wasn't comfortable with, so she didn't have to worry about fighting off his advances. Yes, he still wanted her as much as he did when they were at the river. If not more so. But he wouldn't make her do anything she didn't want to do, and that included him.

"I can't wait to have a soft bed to sleep on tonight," Natalia said. "You wouldn't believe how comfy the beds are in the taverns, Amberly. You won't want to get up in the morning."

"You won't have to wait much longer," Taredd said as they approached the small cluster of buildings. "But I must warn you, they're not all as comfortable as the last one."

"It's still going to be better than that bedroll," she said.

"Debatable," Dain said.

He'd slept on plenty of beds that were far worse than the bedroll he'd picked up for Natalia, but none of them were as comfortable as his bed at home.

God, how he wished he could be back there already, even if only for a few days. He knew he'd want more than a couple of days at home, though. A year wouldn't be long enough after all the years he'd been gone.

A few people stopped to stare as they made their way through the small village, but most carried on without giving them so much as a sideways glance.

Dain was suspicious of everyone, whether they paid them attention or not. After what happened at the last town, Dain wasn't willing to risk letting Amberly out of his sight for a second.

He had a feeling Taredd was going to be exactly the same where Natalia was concerned.

Even though they both assured the females everything would be okay, they couldn't guarantee that would be the case. Any one of the people wandering around could make a move. Dain hoped for the best, but he was prepared for the worst if it should happen.

He certainly wasn't going to get caught looking the other way, like Taredd had.

"Well," Taredd said, pulling the horse to a halt. "We're here."

Dain jumped down and made his way to the back of the cart. Taredd tied off the horse before joining him.

Before Amberly could climb down from the back of the cart, Dain held out his hands so he could help her.

She stared at them for a moment before giving in and taking his offer of help.

He reached up and grabbed her by the waist. Amberly gasped as he effortlessly lifted her off the cart and placed her gently on the ground next to him.

He made sure she was steady on her feet before reluctantly letting go of her.

"Thank you," she said when he released her.

"You're welcome," he said. "Are you okay to walk?"

"Yes," she said.

He still couldn't believe how quickly she'd healed from her injuries. There wasn't a single mark on her, while Natalia still sported a couple of bruises. They were fading, but he could still see yellowy-green marks on Natalia where she'd been injured.

Yes, the medicine he'd given to Amberly had helped, but he'd given exactly the same thing to Natalia. Since they were both Human, it should have worked the same for both of them.

The only answer his mind kept coming back to was she couldn't be completely Human. After catching a glimpse of amber in her eyes at the river, he was leaning more towards her not being Human. But that just threw up even more questions, like what was she? And did she know she wasn't completely Human?

He would have thought she was a Shapeshifter like him, but other than the small glimpse he'd seen in her eyes, there was nothing else about her that gave any indication she was anything other than Human.

"Thank you," Natalia said to Taredd when he helped

her down a moment later.

"You're welcome," he told her.

"Do you need help carrying our stuff inside?" Natalia asked.

"You can help if you'd like to," he said. "But you don't have to. Dain and I are more than capable."

"I'd like to help," she said.

"Okay," Taredd handed her a small bag. "You can carry this one."

Natalia smiled as she took the bag.

"I'd like to help as well," Amberly said.

Dain knew it was pointless arguing with a female when they had their mind set on something, so he handed her a small bag as well and then divided the rest between himself and Taredd.

Once they had everything they needed, they made their way into the tavern. It wasn't the best place they'd stay, but it was far from the worst.

The rickety old building had definitely seen better days. They could barely see through the windows, they were so filthy. Dain bet they hadn't been cleaned in decades, if not longer. Luckily, the inside was in a hell of a lot better condition than the outside, and a hell of a lot cleaner.

The large open room was lined on either side by booths. Smaller tables and chairs were dotted randomly around the centre of the room, and a bar ran nearly the full width of the room with just enough space for a door to one side.

"Wait here," Taredd said when they were all inside. "I

will go check they have rooms available for us."

"Be quick," Dain said. "I'm starving."

"No surprise there," Taredd said before walking away.

"Do we have to stand in the middle of the room while we wait for him?" Natalia asked. "Everyone is watching us."

It hadn't escaped Dain's notice that they had garnered the attention of every single person in the building.

"Let's move over to a booth," he said.

He pointed at an empty booth in the corner so he could see the entire room and both doors.

The smile that crossed Natalia's face made him smile.

"I was hoping you'd say that," she said. "Those seats look really comfy."

"I think anything would look that way after all the time you've spent in the cart," he said. "Especially since you're not used to travelling that way."

"Yeah," she said. "As much as I've liked not having to walk, my arse isn't as happy."

Dain laughed as he followed them over to the booth. "I know what you mean. Being in the front isn't much better. Maybe we could leave the bedroll out next time, but fold it over so it gives you a little more padding."

"Yes, please," Amberly and Natalia said in unison.

They dumped their bags on the table before scooting round the curved bench seat to leave space for him and Taredd. Dain perched on the edge of the seat, facing outward so he could watch what was happening around them.

"Ah, so much better," Natalia moaned as she leaned

back in the seat.

"Tell me about it," Amberly said. "I don't think I've sat on something so comfy in all my life."

Dain had sat on better, but after seeing the inside of one of their bunkers, he didn't point that out.

The only thing that had any padding in the bunker he'd seen, were the mattresses, and even they weren't so good. Bug infested hay bales wrapped in fabric, that's all they were. Not to mention the smell coming from them.

Taredd returned a moment later with a massive grin on his face.

"I take it we're in luck," Dain said.

"Yep," Taredd said, looking pleased with himself. "They have two double rooms available."

"That's good," Dain said.

"Do you want to go up now?" Taredd asked. "Or did you want to get something to eat first?"

"I don't know about you, but I'd rather have something to eat in the rooms," Dain said, looking around the room. "Too many eyes down here."

"Yeah, that's true," Taredd said as he noticed all the people staring at them. "Come on, let's go."

Amberly and Natalia groaned as they scooted off the bench and picked up their bags, but they didn't complain as they followed Taredd over to the door next to the bar. Hidden behind was a staircase that led up to the first floor landing.

At the top of the stairs was a small, thin hallway with half a dozen doors on either side.

"This one's yours," Taredd said as he stopped outside the first door and handed Dain a key with an over-sized fob. The fob had the room number on it. "We're in the room next door."

"Good to know," he said. "I hope the walls are thick."

"I doubt it," Taredd said. "None of the others appear to be, so I can't see the bedrooms being any different."

"Well, keep the noise down then," Dain said. "I'm shattered and I don't want to be kept up by you two all night."

Taredd smirked at Dain before he led Natalia to the next room.

"I don't think you want to go with them," Dain said when Amberly went to follow them.

"Why not?" she asked innocently.

He waited until their door closed behind them before replying. "Because they're going to be busy."

"Doing what?" she asked.

He decided to be blunt to save time. "Fucking."

"Oh," she said, blushing.

"So, you're better off in here with me," he said.

"Um…" she said, looking unsure.

"Don't worry," he told her. "I don't bite."

Holding the door open, he waited patiently for her to decide what she was going to do. Not that she had a choice. He wasn't lying. She really didn't want to go with Taredd and Natalia, not unless she enjoyed watching people fucking.

Dain nearly burst out laughing at the thought. He could just image the look on her face if she walked in on them.

Thankfully, after a moment's hesitation, she took his word for it and walked into their room.

"Are you hungry?" he asked as he followed her in and closed the door.

He was hoping to distract her from the fact there was only one bed in the room. He was surprised she hadn't complained when Taredd announced he'd only got two double rooms.

But he shouldn't have been concerned. As she looked around the room, taking in the large four-poster bed, she didn't seem bothered at all.

"Um… yes," she said, turning back to him.

"What would you like to eat?" he asked.

"I don't know," she said. "I don't know what food there is."

"I'll tell you what," he said, dumping the bags on the bed. "I'll pick something out for you. Wait here, I'll be back in a couple of minutes."

"Okay," she said, sounding unsure.

"Don't worry, you're safe here," Dain said. "I'm not going far, just downstairs to the bar. Plus, Taredd is right next door with Natalia."

"Okay," she said, still sounding unsure.

"And if you don't like the food," he said, trying to lighten the mood. "You can throw it at me."

Amberly giggled. The magical sound warmed his heart, and he couldn't help but smile.

"I'll hold you to that," she said.

"You can do," he said, winking at her before he turned

and walked back out of the room.

Chapter 17

Amberly wasn't overly keen on being alone with Dain in the bedroom, but he was right. She really didn't want to go with Natalia either.

She still couldn't believe Natalia was sleeping with a Demon. But she couldn't say anything. She'd thrown herself at Dain the first and only time they were alone together, which was why she wasn't keen on being alone with him. She didn't trust herself not to do it again.

It was the last thing she ever expected Natalia to do, though. She didn't even know how she could find him attractive. She could understand if he was like Dain, at least he looked Human. Well, all except his eyes, they definitely weren't Human.

Whereas, Taredd had red skin, completely black eyes, and horns sticking out the top of his head. Amberly didn't think she could get passed the horns and red skin to be intimate with him. But Dain? Yeah, she could definitely be intimate with him. The problem was trying to keep her hands off him.

She couldn't stop thinking about Dain. No matter what she tried, the images kept playing out in her mind of their time together at the river.

What made it worse, was the fact she had to fight against her own body. It wanted nothing more than the feel of his skin against hers. To feel of his lips gently brushing against hers.

A shiver raced down her spine at the memory. No matter how much she tried to convince her body that it was a bad idea, it didn't want to listen. The more time she spent with him, the more she wanted him.

It didn't help that he'd kept his promise to teach her and Natalia about the plants and herbs they came across. He took his time and made sure she understood everything he was showing her before they moved on.

She looked around the room while she waited for him to return, hoping it would take her mind off him.

It wasn't a small room, but the large bed made it appear small. It might not have been so dominating if it didn't have four thick posts with heavy fabric hanging from it.

She had to admit, though; the bed looked incredibly comfortable. She couldn't wait to climb under the blankets. She just wished she didn't have to share it with Dain.

Liar! Her subconscious shouted. *Oh, shut up, you.*

Okay, if she was going to be honest with herself, she had to admit that was the part she was looking forward to the most. Curling up next to Dain. Feeling the warmth of his body against hers.

Her mind flooded with indecent images of them in bed together.

Maybe it's not such a good idea after all.

She peeked her head in the bathroom and instantly wanted to run a bath. The claw-foot tub stood against one wall, while a toilet and basin were on the opposite wall.

She really hoped the taps over the bath worked. From the size of the bath, it would take forever to fill with buckets of hot water. She didn't want to wait that long, but she would if she had to.

Stepping into the room, she leaned over the bath and turned on the taps. The excitement that raced through her when water came gushing out, made her squeal in delight.

She couldn't wait to lie back in the bath when it was filled to the rim with hot water. It was all well and good washing in the river on a hot sunny day, but there hadn't been any hot or sunny days since she arrived this side of the mountain.

It's even large enough for two, her mind pointed out as she turned the taps off.

As if her mind had conjured him up, Dain returned a moment later. He smiled at her when she walked out of the bathroom.

"Dinner won't be long," he told her as he closed the

bedroom door behind him.

As soon as he spoke, her body instantly sparked to life. It took every ounce of willpower not to walk over to him and drag his mouth down to hers so she could devour him.

Give it a rest! She told herself sternly before replying. "Okay, thanks."

"You're welcome," he said. "I can't promise it'll taste any good though. They didn't exactly have much to choose from."

"I'm sure it'll be fine," she said, even though she didn't have a clue if it would be.

Her eyes were glued to him as he walked over to the bed and started rummaging through the bags.

"I'm going to wash up quickly before it gets here," he said. "If someone knocks on the door, don't answer it. I'll hear it in the bathroom, so I'll come out when it gets here."

"Don't worry," Amberly said. "I won't be opening any doors."

She wouldn't have answered the door, anyway. After what Natalia said about the Demons taking her from one of these places, she certainly wasn't going to make it easy by opening the door for them.

"That's a shame," he said as he walked towards the bathroom. "I was hoping you might join me."

The last two words echoed in her mind long after he shut the bathroom door.

Oh, God!

The temptation was unreal. A couple of times while

he was in there, she'd caught herself walking towards the bathroom. She had to physically stop herself, especially when she heard the water running as he filled the bathtub.

Get a grip, girl!

She mentally slapped herself as she turned away from the bathroom. Making her way over to the window, she looked down at the small row of buildings.

It was just like the villages she'd read about in books, but instead of it being occupied by Humans, monsters roamed the streets. At a glance, she could see several species of Demon, Fae, Elves, and even a handful of Pixies flying around.

There weren't any Shapeshifters or Vampires that she could see, but they weren't the only ones missing from the party.

She hadn't noticed many buildings as they arrived, so she wondered where they were all coming from. They couldn't possibly just be passing through like she was. Surely, they would have seen more of them along the way, but they hadn't passed anyone. At least, none that she noticed.

The beings milled around as if they didn't have a care in the world. But she supposed they didn't. It wasn't like they had to hide from Humans anymore.

She heard the water splashing as Dain finished washing and climbed out of the bath. Thankfully, she couldn't hear what Natalia and Taredd were doing in the room next door. The walls must be thicker than they first thought. Either that, or Natalia and Taredd were being incredibly quiet.

Amberly laughed in her head at the thought. After spending nearly her entire life living in close quarters with Natalia, she knew first-hand she couldn't be quiet when caught up in the throes of passion.

The only saving grace was that it wasn't often Natalia paired up with anyone. Since there had been little in the way of options, neither of them had hooked up much.

Amberly made a point of not fucking the same people Natalia had been with, which made the pickings even smaller. It had happened once, and that was more than enough.

She'd been mortified when she found out the guy they had both slept with was boasting about it and comparing them. She could still remember how he'd even laughed about it with his friends.

Both she and Natalia had stayed well away from that guy after that, and so had the rest of the women in the group.

Amberly jumped when someone knocked on the door. She spun around in time to see Dain walk out of the bathroom with a towel wrapped around his waist.

"It's only dinner," he told her.

He opened the door, thanked the person on the other side, and then turned around with a tray in his hand. He kicked the door shut behind him before making his way over to the small table at the end of the bed.

Amberly's mouth had gone dry the moment he walked out of the bathroom. But that wasn't the worst of it. Whatever had come over her at the river, was trying to take over her again, and it scared the shit out of her.

She'd never felt so powerless over her own body before, but with Dain, it was like she had lost all control. All she wanted to do was throw herself at him. It took all of her willpower to keep her feet planted firmly where they were.

"Are you okay?" Dain asked.

That was the question, wasn't it? Amberly wasn't so sure she knew the answer.

If nearly losing control and throwing herself at him again was okay, then yes, she was perfectly fine. But she didn't think that was the right answer.

"Um, yeah, I'm fine," she lied.

He stared at her for a moment before nodding his head.

"Tuck in," he said. "I'll be back in a minute."

"Where are you going?" she asked before she could think better of it.

"Just to get some clothes on," he said, giving her that devastating smile of his. "Don't worry, I'm not going anywhere else tonight."

"Okay."

Part of her was over the moon he wasn't leaving her alone. She wouldn't have to worry about being kidnapped with him around. But a small part of her wished he would, if only to give her time to pull herself together.

It was hard enough keeping her hands off him while Natalia and Taredd were with them. It was near impossible now they were alone. Especially with him walking around in nothing but a towel.

Amberly didn't know if she'd be able to hold out until morning without either going stir crazy, or jumping on him.

He didn't seem to mind last time, her mind piped up. *So, maybe he won't mind again.*

Amberly gave herself a mental slap before turning her attention to the tray of food. She had to admit; it didn't look or smell as bad as she thought it might. In fact, some of it looked incredibly tasty. She even recognized and had eaten some of it, so she knew it would taste good.

She'd eaten some of the fruits and berries before, and she knew what bread looked like, though it had been some time since she'd last had any. But there was plenty on the tray she had never seen before. She just hoped it tasted as good as it looked.

Her mouth went from dry to watering at the sight and smell of the food.

"It won't bite," Dain said, making her jump as he came out of the bathroom.

Amberly's head snapped up and her mouth instantly went dry again. Dain stood in a low-slung pair of loose-fitting trousers and nothing else. The fabric of the trousers did little to hide his manhood either.

"What?"

"The food," he pointed to the table. "It won't bite."

"Oh, yeah, I know," she said, dragging her eyes away from him and back to the table. "I just... wasn't sure where to start."

"Anywhere you want," he said. "Whatever you don't eat, I will."

That's good because there was no way she could eat all the food he'd ordered. Especially since she'd lost her appetite for food the moment he walked out in nothing but a towel.

The only thing she was hungry for now was Dain.

"It won't poison you either," he said.

To prove his point, he picked up some bread and began eating it.

Amberly didn't think it was poisonous. It wouldn't make sense for him to poison her after rescuing her from the Vampires. If it had been his plan all along to kill her, then he probably wouldn't have been so tender when dealing with her wounds. And he certainly wouldn't have taken the time to teach her about all the plants and herbs.

Amberly sat on one of the chairs and tried to ignore the fact that Dain was half dressed as he sat on the other side of the table. She managed to eat a few berries and nibble on a bit of bread before she couldn't stomach anymore.

"You need to eat more than that," Dain said when she brushed off her hands and stood up.

"I will do," she said. "I'm just going to have a bath first."

"Okay. There are some clean clothes for you in that bag," he said, pointing to one of the bags on the bed that he carried in.

It was a good job he told her because she was about

to go in the bathroom empty-handed. Admittedly, she would have just put back on the dirty clothes she was wearing.

She wouldn't have left the bathroom in nothing but a towel like he had, and she certainly wouldn't walk around in nothing at all.

It's not like he hasn't seen you naked already, her mind threw at her.

Ignoring what her mind threw at her, she rummaged around in the bag before making a hasty retreat to the bathroom. As soon as the door closed behind her, she leaned back and let out a sigh.

How she was supposed to keep her hands to herself until morning, she didn't know. He wasn't only a Shapeshifter; he was a walking sex god to boot.

A nice hot bath will help distract me, she thought hopefully.

She plugged the hole in the bottom of the bath before turning the taps on. Hot water instantly poured out, filling the bath in minutes.

It was amazing how fast it filled the bath. She was used to spending an hour or two filling a bath half the size just to climb into lukewarm water. Having hot water on tap was a pure luxury.

Impatient, she quickly stripped off and climbed in the bath before it was full. She turned off the taps when the water reached the top of the bath and then leaned back.

She let out a sigh as the hot water worked its magic. Soothing her aching muscles and washing all her troubles away, if only for the moment.

It didn't take long for her mind to drift to the man in the other room. He seemed to consume her thoughts constantly, waking and asleep. No matter what she did, she couldn't get him out of her mind.

Maybe I just need some relief, she thought as she slid one hand under the water and gently touch the bundle of nerves between her legs.

It wasn't the same as having someone else do it for her, but it was better than nothing. And if it helped her gain some kind of control over herself when she around Dain, then she was all for it.

Shifting position slightly, she lifted her feet out of the water and hooked them on either side and then slid down the bath. It wasn't the most dignified position, but it gave her better access.

Slowly, so as not to splash around too much, she slid her hand back under the water to the junction between her legs. Her mind flooded with images of Dain as she began to stroke the bundle of nerves.

She was tentative at first, worried he would hear her, but she soon stopped caring as she was swept up in the moment. The thought of getting caught by him just made her all the hotter.

Her eyes closed on a moan as she slid a finger inside her. As she pumped it in and out, she imagined it was Dain's fingers and hand doing all the work and not hers.

She massaged her breast with her free hand, but it still wasn't enough. She needed... wanted... more.

Before long, water splashed around her as she built up speed with her hand. She was so close to the edge, but no matter what she did, she couldn't tip over.

Amberly was close to crying out in frustration when the bathroom door was thrown open. Her eyes snapped open to see Dain stood in the doorway with a hungry look in his eyes.

His breath came in jagged puffs like her own, and as she looked down his incredible body, she noticed his cock straining beneath his loose-fitting trousers.

Just like at the river, something took over Amberly's mind and body. With a confidence she never knew she had, she let go of her breast and hooked her finger at him.

Dain's eyes were glued to her hand under the water as he stalked over to the bath like a hungry predator ready to devour its prey. She didn't stop pumping her finger in and out until he was towering over her.

Her heart skipped a beat as his tongue slipped out of his mouth and licked his lips.

"Don't stop," he said huskily when she removed her hand.

The desire she saw swimming in his eyes set her blood on fire, so she slid her finger back inside her core.

No man had ever looked at her the same way Dain was looking at her. It made her feel confident and sexy. It made her feel wanted.

Chapter 18

Dain knew it would be hard to keep his hands to himself when he was alone with Amberly, but not once did he doubt that he would be able to.

He was doing fine right up until the food arrived. When he turned around with the tray of food in his hands, the first thing he noticed was the hungry look on Amberly's face, and it had nothing to do with the food on the tray.

Her eyes were glued to his naked chest as he walked towards her and placed the tray on the table at the end of the bed.

Even if he hadn't seen the desire in her eyes, her scent gave her away. It filled the air around him, luring him in for a taste.

If it hadn't been for the fear he'd seen mixed with the

desire in her eyes, he would have dropped the towel and taken her right there and then. But he held back, not wanting to force her into doing something she really didn't want to do.

Thankfully, the fear didn't last for long. By the time he'd put on a pair of loose-fitting trousers and returned to the bedroom, the fear he'd seen in her eyes had disappeared.

The desire in her eyes didn't vanish, and neither did the scent of her arousal. He stupidly thought when she raced off to the bathroom that he'd be able to gain some control over his own body, but that wasn't the case. If anything, it was made worse. Especially when he heard her soft moans through the closed door.

He tried to stay out of the bathroom, he really did. But he had been fighting a losing battle.

Unable to resist any longer, he had swung open the bathroom door and was greeted with the sexiest sight he'd ever seen.

Amberly had her legs splayed as she pumped her fingers in and out of her pussy. She was using her free hand to massage her breast at the same time, and it was the hottest thing he'd ever seen.

He was torn between wanting to watch her bring herself to orgasm and wanting to move her hand out of the way and replace it with his own.

When she opened her eyes and saw him standing there, he expected her to scream at him to leave, or at the least, stop what she was doing and try to cover herself. He certainly hadn't expected her to crook her finger at him, inviting him to join her, but he wasn't going to say no.

As if pulled by a string, he closed the distance in a heartbeat. As he towered over her, she went to remove her finger from her pussy.

"Don't stop," he told her.

A look of uncertainty crossed her features, but was soon transformed into desire as she looked up at him.

Without a word, she continued pleasuring herself.

Dain knelt down next to the bath, so he was closer to the action. He released his cock from his pants and began stroking his length in time with her hand.

With his free hand, he leaned over and began massaging one of her breasts. Instantly, her other hand went to her other breast and mimicked his movements.

"Fuck me," he said huskily. "You're so fucking sexy."

His cock throbbed in his hand as she brought herself closer and closer to climax. Water splashed over the sides of the bath as she built up speed. But she still didn't tip over the edge.

He could see she was getting frustrated by it. So, he released his cock and tucked it back inside his trousers before nudging her hand out of the way.

His finger slid easily inside her. She was so wet, so ready to burst, it wouldn't take much to send her over the edge.

He slowly pumped his finger in and out a couple of times before adding a second and then third finger. He hooked his fingers, putting pressure on her g-spot as he built up speed.

Amberly didn't hold back. She just let go, completely immersing herself in the pleasure.

Her eyes slammed shut and her back arched under the water as she finally exploded around his fingers. She screamed her release to the ceiling.

Nobody could hear her cries of pleasure. He'd found out by the tavern owner that there was a spell in place to make all the rooms soundproof. But even if there wasn't, he didn't care if others heard her.

When her orgasm finally subsided, he removed his fingers and stood up. Grabbing a towel, he held it out for her.

It took Amberly a moment to steady herself on her feet. When she was ready, he wrapped the towel around her body and then picked her up and carried her to the bedroom.

He didn't put her down until he stood next to the bed. Lowering her to her feet, he gently tugged the towel from her and then preceded to dry her hair and body.

Amberly didn't fight him. She stood with her arms and legs spread slightly so he could reach all of her and then turned around so he could dry her back before facing him again.

Once he was done, he dropped the towel to the floor and pulled her into his arms. As he looked into her eyes, he could see the desire he felt reflexed back at him.

"Do you want this?" he asked her.

He hadn't given her the chance to change her mind last time because he'd been so caught up in the moment, but he refused to make that mistake again. He needed to know that she wanted this as much as he did.

It would take every last ounce of willpower he possessed to pull away, but he would do it. For her, he would do anything.

"Yes," she whispered as she wrapped her arms around his neck. "I want this."

"Good," he said, lowering his lips to hers.

He had intended on taking it slow, but as soon as his lips touched hers, he lost the last of his control. His heart raced in his chest as he deepened the kiss.

Grabbing her by the hips, he lifted her up into his arms. Amberly instantly wrapped her legs around his waist. Her moist pussy against his skin set his blood on fire.

Never in his life had he wanted someone as much as he wanted her. He should be concerned by how much power she had over him, but at that moment in time, he didn't care. He relished in it.

Holding Amberly tightly against him, he crawled onto the bed and then lowered her on to her back.

He reached around his back and unhooked her legs. Amberly moaned when he pulled away from her lips, but she stopped as soon as he began trailing kisses down her neck and chest. He stopped long enough to suck each nipple into his mouth and flick his tongue against the tips before continuing.

He nipped and kissed his way down her body, following the soft curves of her abdomen and hips, before finally reaching his prize.

The scent of her arousal was driving him crazy. He'd

been so consumed with needing to be inside her last time, he didn't have the chance to taste her, but he wasn't going to miss the opportunity again.

He couldn't wait another second to taste her. Using his thumbs to spread open her lips, he leaned in and took his first lick.

She tasted like the sweetest ambrosia, coating his tongue and driving him insane. He could see himself getting addicted to the taste of her very quickly if he wasn't careful.

Who was he kidding? He was well and truly addicted to her already, and it had nothing to do with her sweet nectar. He was addicted to everything about her. The more time he spent with her, the more he wanted her.

Amberly's moans of pleasure filled the room as he devoured her with his mouth.

Wrapping his lips around her pussy, he gently sucked as he breached her walls with two fingers. Pushing them in as far as they would go, he twirled them inside her and then crooked his fingers as he pulled them back out.

He repeated the movement over and over until she was thrashing on the bed.

"Please," she begged.

Letting go of her pussy with a loud pop, he asked, "what do you want, baby?"

He didn't stop sliding his fingers in and out of her hot, moist pussy while he waited for her to tell him what she wanted.

"I need," she groaned.

"What do you need?" he asked huskily.

"You," she moaned.

"You have me," he told her, but he knew that wasn't what she meant.

"No!" she said, frustration evident in her voice. "I need you... inside me... now!"

"Okay, baby," he said soothingly. "Anything you want, you can have."

He pumped his fingers inside her two more times before pulling out and crawling back up the bed. He lined up his cock with her entrance and then slowly breached her walls.

The feel of her tight, hot pussy around his cock was heaven on earth. As soon as he was fully seated, he held still for a moment so she could adjust to his size. When he felt her relax around him, he began to slowly pull out until only the tip was inside her.

He gently brushed his lips against hers and then licked the seam, asking her without words to open for him. She did instantly. As he slipped his tongue in her mouth to duel with hers, he pushed his cock all the way in again.

He repeated the move over and over, building up speed with each inward thrust as he devoured her mouth. Licking, sucking, and nipping on each other's tongues and lips.

Before long, he was pounding in and out of her as hard and fast as he could. Both of them were hurtling towards climax, but he wasn't ready for it to be over with just yet.

Pulling out of her, he spun them both around until she was straddling his lap.

Amberly gasped at the sudden movement, but she didn't complain about the new position. Instead, she rested her hands on his chest so she could brace herself before she began moving.

She started off slowly, gently grinding against him. Her breasts swayed with her movements, tempting him. Unable to resist, he reached up with both hands and cupped each breast.

He brushed his thumbs over the tight nipples, eliciting a moan of pleasure from Amberly. So, he did it a couple more times before gently pinching them between his thumb and forefinger. Amberly arched her back, pushing her breasts further into his hands.

He let go of one of her breasts and placed his hand on her back to steady her as he sat up. Before she had a chance to complain about the loss of his touch on her nipple, he sucked it into his mouth. Scrapping his teeth against the sensitive tip before licking it.

Amberly moaned as her hands went to the back of his head, holding him against her as she rocked back and forth on his cock. He moved from one breast to the other, paying each the same amount of attention.

She seemed unsure of herself at first, but it didn't take her long to gain confidence. After a few minutes, Amberly gently pushed him back on the bed and placed her hands on his chest again.

She stopped rocking against him. Using his chest to help brace her, she began slowly bouncing up and down on his cock.

Her breasts bounced with her, teasing him even more,

but he did as she wanted and stayed lying on his back.

Amberly soon got into a rhythm, bouncing up and down as fast as she could.

A light sheen of sweat coated her skin, making it glisten in the candlelight. At that moment in time, he was glad he'd lit the candles and closed the curtains when she first got in the bath.

Just as he felt her begin to slow, he spun them around, placing her once again on her back beneath him.

He took control of her mouth. Showing her in that one kiss how much she meant to him before he lost control and began pounding inside her. This time he didn't stop until they both tipped over the edge.

Dain roared as hot jets of come shot out of him, filling her with his seed. At the same time, Amberly closed her eyes and threw her head back into the mattress as she screamed her orgasm to the heavens.

The urge to mark her as his was so much stronger than it had been at the river. He bit down hard on his lip, drawing blood just to stop himself from mating with her.

As soon as they were both finished, he pulled out of her hot pussy and laid down next to her. Wrapping an arm around her waist, he pulled her towards him so her back was against his chest.

Neither of them uttered a word as their breathing slowly down and their hearts stopped racing. He held her tightly against him as she drifted off to sleep in his arms.

A million thoughts raced through Dain's mind, preventing him from drifting off with her. The one that was screaming loudest, was the one telling him she was his and to mate with her.

He could have sworn he caught a glimpse of glowing amber in her eyes again, but until he could be one hundred per cent sure that she was one of his kind, he couldn't mate with her, no matter how much he wanted to.

He decided there and then that next time... because there would be a next time, he was certain of that... he was going to make sure she kept her eyes open and locked with his.

He'd been lucky so far, but he couldn't guarantee he would be able to hold back from mating with her. Sooner or later, the urge was going to be too strong for him to resist.

So, he needed to know for sure if she was one of his kind. He didn't think asking her would produce an answer either, because he had a feeling she didn't know if she was a Shapeshifter. Or at least, part Shapeshifter.

No, the only way he was going to know for sure was by seeing it in her eyes as she climaxed. He was more than ready to make that happen again, but Amberly needed to rest. She hadn't slept much since she was rescued, so he didn't want to wake her.

Morning would arrive soon enough and then he would know, one way or another.

Chapter 19

Amberly woke to the most delicious sensations tingling through her body. She arched her back and reached up for the headboard as she stretched the top half of her body before opening her eyes.

She couldn't stretch her legs out because they were being held open. As she looked down at the bed, she could see Dain's head bobbing under the covers as he devoured her.

She moaned as he flicked his tongue over the bundle of nerves and breached her walls with his talented fingers. She could certainly get used to being woken up that way.

His tongue was like magic. Bringing her to life in seconds as he slowly slid his finger in and out.

She leaned her head back into the pillow and closed

her eyes. Concentrating on the feel of his fingers and tongue, she tried to picture what he was doing in her mind, but it didn't work. All she could think about was sliding his cock in her mouth.

She wanted to know what he felt like against her tongue. She wanted to know what he tasted like. But more importantly, she wanted to return the favour, showing him the same pleasure he was giving her.

Amberly had only ever willingly done that once before, and she hadn't enjoyed it. Since then, she hadn't wanted to do it with anyone else. She didn't have a choice with the Vampires. They made her do plenty of things she didn't want to do.

She didn't want to think about her time with them at that moment in time. So, she quickly chased away all thoughts of the Vampires and concentrated on Dain and his talented hands and mouth.

With Dain, she wanted to give him as much pleasure as he was giving her. And if that meant taking his cock into her mouth, she would do it, willingly.

He added another finger inside her, stretching her deliciously, before he began building up speed. He didn't let up on his attack on her bundle of nerves with his tongue.

As his fingers pumped in and out of her, they rubbed against one spot inside her continuously. Whatever he was doing, it was hurtling her towards climax.

Amberly squirmed uncontrollably on the bed. She tried to close her legs on him, unable to take anymore, when she suddenly shot over the edge. Wave after wave of pure pleasure hit her until she didn't know when one stopped and another started.

She didn't have a clue what he'd done, but it was like the floodgates had opened. Never in her life had she had such an intense orgasm.

She never thought she would be a screamer like some of the other woman she'd lived with in the bunkers either, but Dain had managed to make her scream not once, but twice now. She was just glad she hadn't screamed her release when they were by the river.

That would have been the ultimate embarrassment because there was no way Natalia and Taredd wouldn't have heard her. She would be amazed if they hadn't heard her through the walls, but at least it would be slightly muffled through the walls compared to being out in the open.

Dain continued pumping his fingers in and out of her until the waves started to ebb. Only then did he pull his fingers out of her and crawl up the bed.

"Morning, beautiful," he said huskily.

"Morning."

She was amazed her voice came out as clearly as it did after all the screaming she'd done.

"I hope you didn't mind me waking you up," he said. "But I needed to taste you again."

Amberly's heart skipped a beat at his words and the desire she saw in his eyes as he looked down at her. She definitely didn't mind him waking her up like that. He could do it more often as far as she was concerned.

"I don't mind," she said, smiling at him.

"Good," he said. "Because I plan on doing it again."

As he spoke, Dain slid his hand down her body to cup her between the legs. Just as he was about to press his fingers inside her again, she moved his hand out of the way and gently pushed against his shoulder until he was on his back.

Dain looked at her questioningly.

"I want to return the favour," she told him as she crouched next to him.

"You don't have to," he told her.

"I know," she said with a small smile. "I want to."

"Okay," he said, smiling back.

"Just... do me one favour?" she asked.

"Anything you want," he said.

"Don't touch my head," she said. "I mean, don't hold the back of my head."

Thankfully, he didn't ask why, he just nodded his head in agreement.

"I promise," he said.

With one last smile, she shuffled down the bed until she was level with his cock.

She took hold of him in her hand. His silky soft skin was such a contrast to how hard he was.

She glided her hand up, and down his length, changing the speed and pressure of her grip. She watched his reactions as she learnt what he did and didn't like.

She loved the way his cock twitched in her hand when she did something he enjoyed. Her confidence was bolstered by the look of desire she saw on his face when she peeked up at him.

Eager for a taste, she leaned over him, pulling the covers with her. It was one thing having him watch her stroke his length, but it was completely different having him watch her take his cock into her mouth. She definitely wasn't ready for that yet.

As soon as she was hidden by the blanket, she took a deep breath and then leaned in for a tentative lick. Holding his cock with one hand, she swiped her tongue over the tip where a drop of pre-come sat waiting for her.

That small taste of him filled her mouth, instantly making her want more. The sound of Dain's moan set her blood on fire and encouraged her on.

She flicked and twirled her tongue on the tip before wrapping her lips around the head. He twitched in her mouth, but she still had hold of him, so he couldn't move too much.

She lowered her head slowly, taking him as far into her mouth as she could. She held still for a second before sliding him back out and repeating the movement.

Not even half of him fit inside her mouth on the first go. But, with each downward stroke, she was able to take more of him. She still wasn't able to take all of him because he was just too big, but she took as much as she could without choking.

To make up the difference, she used the hand holding him in place to gently stroke up and down his length in time with her mouth.

It didn't take long for her to find her rhythm. Her hand and mouth were moving in unison to bring him closer to the edge.

She knew it was working because he kept tensing up underneath her as more drops of pre-come coated her mouth to mix with her saliva.

Dain kept his word and didn't touch her head, but he couldn't stop his hips from moving. She could tell he was trying his hardest not to choke her by pushing too far into her mouth, but he couldn't stop from lifting his hips slightly whenever she took his cock to the back of her throat.

Dain's voice came out strained when he said, "Amberly, you need to stop."

"Why?" she asked.

Not wanting to stop what she was doing; the word came out muffled as she spoke around his length.

"Because I'm going to come if you continue," he growled.

Amberly didn't bother stopping. She wanted to taste all of him, just like he'd done with her. He hadn't stop licking and sucking her when she came, so she wasn't going to either.

Instead, she moaned around him. A second later, he roared as hot jets of come shot down her throat. She swallowed every drop of him, not wanting to waste any.

When he was finished, she crawled back up the bed to lie down next to him. But before she had the chance to lie down, he pounced on her. Flipping her on to her back, he wedged his hips between her legs.

Amberly gasped at the sudden movement. She could feel the tip of his cock pressed against her entrance.

"Don't you need some time to rest first?" she asked.

The few people she'd taken to her bed had needed at least an hour after they came before they were ready to go again. So, she had expected Dain to be the same.

"Does it feel like I need time to rest first?" he asked, pushing the tip inside her.

"No," Amberly moaned.

She was glad he wasn't like her past partners. More often than not, she'd been left wanting after they'd finished.

"I could go all night," he whispered in her ear. "Especially with you."

Before she could reply, he slid the rest of the way inside her. After that, words completely failed her. She couldn't even think of a reply because all thought left as sensation took over.

Amberly's toes curled as Dain took her mouth in a passionate kiss. Wrapping her arms and legs around him, she held on tight as he slowly slid his cock in and out of her.

It was so completely different from the other times she had been with him, that it brought tears to her eyes. So soft and gentle, caring and intimate, it took her breath away.

He was showing her a whole other side to him, and she liked it. No, she loved it.

With every slow movement, every gently caress, her heart melted a little more for him. If he kept it up, she was afraid she'd never get him out of her heart again.

But she didn't stop him. She couldn't. Somehow, he'd

already found his way inside her heart, and it didn't look like that was going to change anytime soon, if ever.

She felt bereft when he broke the kiss. She didn't want the night to end, but she knew it would. Dawn had already broken; she knew their time together would soon come to an end.

She tried to hold off the orgasm she could feel building, but it was in vain.

"Look at me," he whispered softly.

She knew it would be a big mistake to look at him, but she couldn't deny him.

"You are so beautiful," he said, gently brushing a strand of hair off her face. "Don't close your eyes."

Amberly couldn't bring herself to speak. He could already see the tears trailing down her cheeks, he didn't need to hear her voice break as well. So, she just nodded her head and kept her eyes locked with his.

Even if she wanted to, she didn't think she could look away. Up close, his glowing amber eyes were even more beautiful.

Held captive by those stunning eyes of his, she had no choice but to see the emotions play out across his face. Lust, desire, happiness, it was all laid bare for her to see, along with love.

The love she saw in his eyes scared her more than anything else, because it was reflexing exactly how she felt. She wasn't scared to be loved. She was scared that she was wrong about seeing it in his eyes.

Her heart swelled with hope as she climbed closer to the edge. She cried out his name as she tipped over the edge, he followed her a moment later.

She thought the last orgasm he'd given her was intense, but this one blew it out of the water. It felt like her soul was reaching out to join with his. Mixing them together until she didn't know where he left off and she began.

What alarmed her most was the urge to bite down on his neck. It was so strong, she had to bite down on her own lip to stop from following through with it.

When the waves finally subsided, she looked at Dain's mouth to see that he was doing the same thing.

He froze for a moment, his eyes widening as he stared down at her. She couldn't make out what emotion was playing out across his face, but she didn't think it was good.

"What's the matter?" she asked, concern filling her and turning her blood cold.

"Nothing," he said, finally blinking. "Nothing at all, baby."

When he smiled, the lump that had appeared in her stomach shrank a little, but didn't disappear completely. She didn't know what he'd seen in her eyes, but she couldn't shake the feeling that something was wrong and he just wasn't telling her.

He leaned down and placed a kiss on the tip of her nose before pulling out of her so he could lie down next to her. Wrapping an arm around her waist, he pulled her against him.

She rested her head on his chest and listened to his heart beating. It was comforting to know it was beating just as fast as hers.

"Do you think they heard us?" she finally plucked up the courage to ask.

She dreaded to think what Natalia and Taredd had heard last night and this morning. She had to admit though; she was grateful she hadn't heard them.

"No, they wouldn't have heard us," he said. "Just like we haven't heard them."

"How?" she asked.

Not that she wanted them to hear, but she couldn't understand how they wouldn't have. She screamed pretty loudly at times. She wouldn't be surprised if the whole damn building had heard her.

"Each room has a spell in place to make them sound-proof," he told her as if she was meant to understand what he meant.

"Huh?"

"The owner of the building had a Witch cast a spell on each of the rooms," he explained. "So, it doesn't matter how much noise we make, nobody can hear us unless they are in the room with us." When her eyes widened at the thought of someone being in the room with them, he added; "Trust me, we are alone in here. I would know if we weren't."

"That's good to know," she said. "Is that why we didn't hear them either?"

"Yes, thank God," he said. "I really don't want to listen to what they're doing."

"Me neither," she said. "So, I'm definitely not com-plaining. Are all taverns like this?"

"How do you mean?"

"With spells cast on the rooms."

"No, not all of them unfortunately," he said. "But the good ones are."

"I'm glad we stopped here then," she said.

"So am I," he agreed.

Amberly didn't want to move. She didn't want to get up and face the world outside of their room. She wanted this moment to last forever, just her and Dain in their own little cocoon. But she knew all too soon she would have to get up and face the outside world.

Chapter 20

As much as Dain didn't want to move from the bed, he needed to speak with Taredd about Amberly.

After that morning's activities, there was no doubt in his mind she was a Shapeshifter. It was the only explanation for the glowing amber eyes. He just didn't understand why they only glowed during sex. Or more precisely, as she climaxed.

The rest of the time, her eyes were a light blue. They were a stunning light blue, but they certainly didn't glow.

It would also explain why the Vampires hadn't killed her like they had the others. They would have been addicted to the taste of her blood, so they would have wanted to keep her alive for as long as possible.

It also meant he was right about them not letting her

go easily. Once a Vampire had tasted the blood of a Shapeshifter, they would do anything and everything to get more of it, but only from the same Shapeshifter they had already tasted.

It was both a blessing and a curse that they only craved the blood they had already tasted. They never targeted just any random Shapeshifter, which was part of the blessing. If the Vampire was killed straight away, it wasn't a problem either. But if they weren't, they would let nothing stand in their way as they ruthlessly hunted down their target.

Dain held Amberly a little tighter at the thought of a horde of Vampires ruthlessly hunting her down. They didn't know the exact number of Vampires that drank from her, but it wouldn't surprise him if all the Vampires at the campsite came after her.

From the size of the campsite, it would mean a hell of a lot of Vampires would be coming after her, possibly more than Dain and Taredd could handle on their own.

Let them try taking her from me!

It didn't matter how many came after her, he would never let any of them get close enough to harm her, and he certainly wouldn't let them take her away from him. But he still didn't like the idea of her being hunted.

"We need to get up soon," he said reluctantly.

Amberly moaned, "do we have to?"

Dain smiled. He could happily spend the entire day in bed with her, but he knew they couldn't.

"Unfortunately, we have to," he said, kissing the top of her head. "I need to speak with Taredd about what supplies we're going to need, and then I'll have to pick them up before we can get on the road again."

"Okay," she sighed. "I suppose you're right. Are we staying here another night? Or are we leaving today?"

"I'm not sure," he said.

It would be wise to leave straight away so they could keep some distance between them and the Vampires. But he didn't want to worry her, so he kept it to himself.

"I hope we can stay for one more night," she said. "I've never slept in a bed so comfortable before."

"I've seen some of the beds you've slept on," he said. "I certainly wouldn't want to sleep on any of them. In fact, it would probably be more comfortable to sleep on the floor."

"You're right, none of them were very comfortable," she agreed. "But it was warmer than sleeping on the floor."

"There's that, I suppose," he said.

Dain didn't care if they were warmer than sleeping on the floor, he would have still chosen the floor. The smell alone was more than enough to put him off using them.

"How many of the bunkers have you seen inside of?" she asked.

"Just the one," he told her. "But that was more than enough. I don't know how you lived down there for so long."

"We didn't exactly have much of a choice," she said. "If we weren't being hunted and killed, then we wouldn't have needed to live in a hole in the ground."

Guilt ate at Dain. He was the reason she had no choice

but to live underground in a bunker. He wasn't the only one, and neither were Taredd and Arun, but they played a big part in how Amberly's life had been so far.

"I'm sorry," he said.

Amberly shifted position so she could lean on her elbow and look at him.

"It wasn't your fault," she told him. "You didn't start the war, did you?"

"Well, no," he said. "But I did other things."

"I know," she said. "I'm not stupid. I know you and Taredd have killed my kind."

"And that doesn't bother you?" he asked.

Dain dreaded the answer, but the question was out before he could think better of it, and now there was no taking it back. He couldn't do anything to change the past, but he could try to make up for it in the future. And that's exactly what he planned to do.

Amberly was silent for a moment. He could see she was thinking about her answer.

"What can I do about it?" she finally replied. "It's not as if I can change the past. If I could, I would make sure there wasn't a war in the first place."

"But then we wouldn't have met," he said, not liking the idea of never meeting her.

"You never know, we might still have met," she said. "Just under different circumstances."

"Yeah, maybe."

He liked the thought of meeting her under different circumstances, but he knew it wouldn't have been the case. It was because of the war and him hunting her kind that ultimately led to their meeting. If it hadn't been for either of those reasons, he would still be in the Shifter realm.

He certainly wouldn't be living among the Humans, hiding his true identity. He knew plenty of Shapeshifters had lived among them before the Great War, but it had never appealed to him.

Before either of them could say any more on the subject, there was a knock on the door.

"Looks like our time is up," he said.

"I know," she said, sounding sad.

Just as Amberly was about to turn away from him and climb out of bed, he stopped her by gently placing a hand under her chin and turning her face towards him.

"Our time is up, for now," he told her when she was looking at him. "But it isn't the end, I promise you that."

No, he definitely wasn't finished with her, or their conversation. But they did need to get up. He needed to speak with Taredd about what their next move was going to be.

Dain placed a gently kiss on her lips just as the knock on the door came again.

"One minute," he shouted.

"I thought you said nobody could hear us in here?" she asked.

"True," he said, grinning. "He'll just have to wait without knowing then, won't he?"

Amberly giggled. He loved the sound and wanted to hear more of it, but it would have to wait. There were more important things he needed to be getting on with.

"Aren't you going to put some clothes on first?" she asked as he climbed out of bed and headed straight for the door.

"Na, Taredd's seen my naked ass plenty of times," he told her.

"Yeah, but he might not be alone," she reminded him.

"Oh, shit," he said. "I forgot about Natalia for a moment."

Amberly giggled again as she watched him race back over to the bed. He quickly pulled on the trousers he had on last night before returning to the door.

"You took your time answering the door," Taredd said as soon as the door was opened.

"Good morning to you too," Dain said pointedly.

"Yes, good morning to you both," Taredd said as he looked past Dain into the room. "I hope you slept well, Amberly, and that Dain didn't keep you up all night with his snoring?"

"I slept really well, thank you," Amberly said. "And I didn't hear any snoring."

"I don't snore as loud as you," Dain told him. "And as you can see, we were still in bed, that's why it took so long."

A knowing grin crossed Taredd's face. "I had a feeling that might be case."

"I'm surprised you're up and about," Dain said. "I thought you would still be in bed with Natalia."

"Unfortunately not," he said. "She wants to check in and see how Amberly is today. Plus, I only booked the rooms for one night."

As much as Dain wanted to stay for a second night, he was glad Taredd had only booked the rooms for one.

"Ah, I see," he said. "So, where is Natalia?"

"She's having a bath while I grab some breakfast," he told them. "I wasn't sure if you two would be up yet, so I told her I would give you a shout on my way past to make sure you were."

"Why, isn't that nice of you to come take our breakfast orders," Dain said, knowing full well that wasn't the reason.

"No, I haven't come for that," Taredd said adamantly. "I came to check you were up before bring Natalia."

Dain ignored Taredd's comment as he looked over his shoulder at Amberly.

"Amberly, Taredd wants to know what you want for breakfast," Dain said.

"That's nice of him," she said.

Dain could see the smile on her face and the twinkle in her eyes as she spoke. He knew she could easily hear their conversation at the door, so she knew Taredd wasn't there for that, but she replied as if she hadn't been listening to them.

"What would you like?" he asked.

"Um, I don't know," she said, taping her finger against her bottom lip as if thinking about it. "I'll let you choose."

Dain turned back to Taredd with a massive grin on his face.

"Fine," Taredd relented. "I'll order your breakfast as well. But I'm not bringing it to you."

"Cheers," Dain said with a smile.

He rattled off a long list of food before finishing off with a drinks order.

"Anything else?" Taredd asked sarcastically when he was finished.

"Nope, that'll do nicely," he said.

"Fine," Taredd said. "I'll get it sent to your room. Just, make sure you're both dressed when I come back with Natalia."

"Will do," Dain said as he closed the door.

Amberly was sitting on the bed with the blanket tucked tightly around her when he turned around.

"Well, we've got some time to kill before the food arrives," he said. "What do you fancy doing?"

He knew exactly what he wanted to be doing while they waited for breakfast to arrive. And luckily for him, Amberly was thinking the same thing.

She threw off the blanket, exposing her naked body to him, before leaning back on the bed with her legs spread. She looked at him from between her legs and crooked her finger at him.

"Well, I certainly won't say no to that," he told her as he strolled over to the bed.

Gently wrapping his hands around her ankles, he pulled her towards him until her ass was balanced on the edge of the bed.

"I'll never say no to you," he said huskily.

Which was the truth. All she had to do was say the word and he would come running. Even if she wasn't lying there completely naked with desire swimming in those beautiful blue eyes of her, he wouldn't be able to say no to her.

"So fucking beautiful," he said before leaning down to take her mouth in a fiery kiss.

He wanted to see those glowing amber eyes of hers as she climax for him again. They didn't have long, but what little time they did have, he was going to make count.

Chapter 21

She didn't know what it was about Dain, but she couldn't keep her hands off him.

I've had more sex in the last twenty-four hours than I've had in the last four years.

Amberly smiled at the thought as she relaxed in the bath. Her body deliciously sore in all the right places.

She couldn't believe how brazen she was around him. It was like all the barriers she'd kept up around men over the years had just suddenly crumbled into nothing. But only for him, only for Dain.

"Amberly," Dain shouted through the door. "Taredd and Natalia are here."

Thankfully, she had already washed her hair and body. She was just enjoying the bath so much that she didn't want to get out.

"Okay, I'll be out in a minute," she shouted back, not wanting to move.

She looked at the towel on the other side of the room and decided it could stay exactly where it was for the moment.

Another minute or two won't hurt.

After all, she didn't know when she'd be able to have another bath like she was having now. The next place they stopped at might not have hot water on tap, so she wasn't going to let the hot water she'd already run go to waste.

Admittedly, she should have had a bath earlier like Natalia, but she hadn't been able to resist Dain. The way he'd stood blocking the doorway with those loose-fitting trousers on and nothing else had set her blood on fire.

He needs to stop wearing those trousers.

It was hard enough keeping her hands to herself at the best of times, but it was impossible when he looked at her like he wanted to devour her. Even from across the room, she'd been able to see the desire swimming in his eyes when he looked at her.

She didn't regret a single second of their time together, but she did wish it didn't have to come to an end so soon. If she had her way, they wouldn't be leaving the room, or the bed, for at least a couple of days.

Unfortunately, it wasn't up to her. It was up to Dain and Taredd when they would be leaving, and from what Taredd had said at the door earlier, they would be leaving today.

It wouldn't be long before they left the sanctuary of the bedroom behind as continued on their journey.

She couldn't imagine they would get much alone time while they were travelling. But then again, Natalia and Taredd had tried to sneak off on their own, and they would have been successful if it hadn't been for her.

Well, at least they didn't have to worry about her getting in the way anymore. If it meant she would get to spend some time alone with Dain, then she was all for letting them wander off on their own.

As she climbed out of the bath, her mind went over the conversation she had with Dain earlier that morning.

He'd surprised her by apologizing for the way she'd been forced to live her life. She wasn't naïve; she knew his hands weren't clean. He'd hunted down and killed her kind just like the rest of them.

It should bother her, and it did to an extent, but not as much as she thought it would.

He didn't start the war that unleashed all hell on earth. She didn't know what did, but she couldn't see it starting because of one person. And she couldn't see him being the one to start the slaughtering of her kind either.

Yes, he wasn't innocent, but then neither were Humans. They had nearly destroyed the planet before the war broke out, and they had killed more than their fair share of innocent creatures because of their own greed.

The amount of animal and plant life that no longer existed because of Humans, was more than she could count on her hands and toes. And that was just the ones she'd read about. God knows how many more had gone extinct that weren't recorded in the books she'd come across.

So, she didn't blame Dain and the rest of them for wanting to see the end of the Human race. She would've wanted to do the same if she was in their position.

Probably not to the same extent, but if she had the abilities they had, she would do everything in her power to put a stop to all the death and destruction as well.

None of them could change the past, so there was no point dwelling on it. All they could do was try to make a better future for everyone.

Amberly wonder what had changed. Why weren't they hunting and killing Humans anymore?

She had a feeling she already knew the answer. Natalia. They had stopped because Taredd had fallen for Natalia.

But was it all Humans they had stopped hunting and killing? Or was it just her and Natalia that had a free pass? Amberly was scared to know the answer.

As much as she was falling for Dain, she wouldn't be able to look past him still murdering her kind. She couldn't change the past, but that didn't mean she would stick her head in the sand while it continued in the future.

It would break her heart to leave, but she would walk away. Even if it meant going alone.

As soon as she was dry, she quickly pulled on clean clothes. She wrapped her hair in the towel and then join the others in the bedroom.

"They're good, aren't they?" Natalia asked as soon as

she stepped out of the bathroom.

"What?" Amberly tensed as panic set in that Natalia had heard them last night after all.

"The bath," she laughed. "They're really good, aren't they? It's amazing having hot water on tap. I've never had a bath so hot before."

"Oh, yeah, me neither," Amberly said as she let out a sigh of relief. "I could spend all day in there."

"Tell me about it," Natalia agreed. "I would still be in there, but Taredd said we need to go soon."

"First, we need to pick up more supplies," Taredd said.

"Yeah, yeah, I know," Natalia said as she waved away his words with her hand. "But that doesn't involve me or Amberly. You already said we'd be staying here."

Amberly didn't like the idea of staying in the tavern without Dain and Taredd being with them. Especially after they told her what happened the last time Natalia was alone in one.

Vampires were bad enough, I don't fancy getting kidnapped by a bunch of Demons as well, she thought.

"Don't worry," Dain said, reading her mind. "You won't be alone. Taredd's staying with you while I get everything we need."

"Okay," she said, smiling.

She would prefer Dain to stay with them, but she supposed Taredd was better than nobody.

"It'll give us some time to chat, and for you to eat," Natalia said as she pointedly looked at the tray of food. "It doesn't look as if you've touched your breakfast."

Amberly's stomach growled loudly, confirming Natalia was right. After the night she had, she was hungry enough to eat a horse. Not that she would ever eat a horse.

"It arrived while Amberly was in the bath," Dain said, saving her from explaining why she hadn't eaten.

It arrived long before she got in the bath, but she wasn't going to tell Natalia.

Amberly could feel her cheeks heating as the memory of what she was doing when it arrived flashed in her mind.

"Well, you've got plenty of time now," Natalia said.

"I shouldn't be long," Dain said.

"Aren't you eating first?" she asked.

"I had some while you were in the bath," he told her. "So the rest is for you."

Amberly looked at the mound of food on the tray. There was no way she could eat it all.

"Are you two hungry?" she asked Natalia and Taredd.

"No," Natalia said, shaking her head at the same time. "We've eaten already."

"Well, I can't eat all of it," she said. "And it seems a waste to leave it."

"Whatever you don't eat," Dain said, kissing her on the forehead. "We'll pack up and take with us."

That sounded like a much better idea than throwing it away, and it meant she wouldn't feel so guilty for not eating it all. "Okay."

"Right, I'll be back soon," Dain said as he walked towards the door.

"See you soon," Natalia said as she waved goodbye.

Amberly heard him whisper to Taredd as he walked past. "Keep them safe."

"I will do," Taredd whispered back.

Natalia, completely unaware Dain and Taredd had said anything as Dain left the room, started talking about the bedroom she and Taredd had stayed in. Amberly nodded along as she half listened to her while she grabbed a plate of food and sat on the end of the bed.

As soon as she took her first bite, her mouth exploded with flavour. She couldn't help closing her eyes as she savoured the mouth-watering taste.

God, how she wished she could eat food like that for the rest of her life. She'd never eaten anything like it in her life.

"It's good, isn't it?" Natalia asked.

"Mmm," was Amberly's only reply.

"Taredd said it's not far off what they have in his realm," Natalia told her. "He was telling me all about his realm last night. I can't wait to see it."

Amberly still wasn't sure she wanted to go to the Demon realm with them. Maybe for a visit, but she couldn't imagine living there.

She loved Natalia like a sister, but she didn't want to live with her and Taredd. She would constantly feel like the third wheel if she lived with them.

If she had a choice in the matter, she would rather live with Dain in the Shapeshifter realm. It didn't even have to be in his home realm. As long as she was with him, she would live anywhere.

Unfortunately, it wasn't down to her. Yes, Dain said he wasn't finished with her, but that didn't mean he wanted to spend the rest of his life with her. Or her life, as the case may be.

"We'll have our own rooms," Natalia beamed as she talked. "It'll be so nice not having to share a room anymore."

Taredd coughed to get Natalia's attention.

"Well, apart from me," she amended as she smiled at him. "I'll be sharing with Taredd."

"What's going on between you two?" The words were out of her mouth before she could think better of it.

"What do you mean?" Natalia asked.

"I know you've had sex," she said. "But is that all she is to you? A quick fuck?"

"Amberly!" Natalia snapped.

"It's okay," Taredd said to Natalia. "She's your friend, and she's looking out for you."

"Yes, I am," Amberly agreed.

She cared for Natalia and didn't want her to get hurt. On the outside, Natalia was a strong woman and could handle anything life threw at her. But Amberly knew that deep down, she had a soft heart that could easily be broken.

Amberly had seen Natalia with a broken heart from a guy before, it had destroyed her confidence and self-esteem. She didn't want to see her go through it again.

"To answer your question," Taredd said to her. "Natalia is my mate."

Natalia smiled as she agreed with him. "Yes, I'm his

mate."

"What does that mean?" she asked. "That she's your friend?"

"It's similar to being husband and wife," Taredd told her.

She knew what a husband and wife were, but his answer still raised more questions than it answered.

"I see," she said. "But don't you live forever?"

The massive age gap was something that had played on her mind a lot. The thought of growing old and dying while Dain stayed looking the same left a hollow feeling in her heart.

As much as she tried to convince herself that it wasn't a problem, she knew it was. After all, she could only be a part of Dain's life for a few short years. She couldn't see why he would want anything more than sex from her when he knew he could only have her for such a short time.

"Yes, that's right," Taredd agreed.

"But, Natalia doesn't," she pointed out. "Eventually, she's going to grow old and die. Doesn't that bother you?"

"You're right," he agreed. "That would normally be the case."

"And that doesn't bother you?" she asked.

"Of course it does," he said.

"So, wouldn't it make more sense for you to mate with one of your own kind?" she asked.

Natalia was silent for once, which made Amberly wonder if they had already spoken about it.

"That isn't how it works," he explained. "Unlike Humans, we don't choose who we are mated with. That is left to fate to decide."

Amberly wasn't sure she believed in fate, but she was willing to keep an open mind for Natalia's sake.

"Okay," she said. "So, when she dies, will you take another mate? Or will you live the rest of your life alone?"

"I wouldn't take another mate," he said.

"So you would spend the rest of your life alone?" she asked sceptically.

"If it came to it, yes, I would live the rest of my life alone," he said. "But I'm hoping that won't be the case, which is why we are looking for Arun."

"I don't understand," she said. "What does your friend have to do with it?"

"His magick can make Natalia immortal."

Those six little words filled her heart with hope.

"How?" she asked eagerly.

She was intrigued to know how it would work. Because, if it worked for them, maybe it could work for her and Dain.

That's if he even wants you as a mate, her mind threw at her.

Yes, it all depended on whether Dain would want her as a mate. He might only see her as convenient fuck for all she knew.

"He will tie her life to mine," he said.

"How?"

"What's with all the questions, Amberly?" Natalia

227

asked.

"I'm just curious to know how it'll work between you," she said. "I'm sorry if I've overstepped at all, I was just wondering."

"It's okay," Taredd said. "Ask your questions."

"How will he tie her life to yours?" she asked. "And how do you know he'll be able to do it?"

"To be honest, I don't know," he said. "But if anyone can, it will be him."

"You have a lot of faith in him," she said.

"I've known him for a very long time."

She could just imagine. After all, he was over three hundred years old.

"I take it he's as old as you and Dain," she said.

"Actually, he's older," he said, surprising her and Natalia.

"Really?" they asked in unison.

"How much older?" Natalia asked.

"By about a thousand years."

"Shit," Amberly breathed. "That's fucking old."

Taredd chuckled. "I'll make sure to tell him you said that."

Embarrassment burned her cheeks as hope took hold of her heart. If Arun could turn Natalia into an immortal by tying her life to Taredd's, then there was hope for her as well.

Chapter 22

Thankfully, since it was only a small village, it didn't take Dain long to roundup everything they needed. There was one or two items he couldn't get, but he was able to pick up the essentials and a new bedroll for Amberly.

As much as she told them she was fine sleeping on the floor, he wasn't happy for her to sleep there without something better to lie on.

Unfortunately, he'd garnered the attention of a few people along the way. He wasn't concerned about most of them, they were just curious about the newcomers in their village.

But there were a couple of people that had followed him around for most of the day.

He could tell they were trying to be inconspicuous

as they watched him, but they failed drastically. They also knew what he was because they made sure to stay upwind from him the entire time.

Dain didn't let on that he knew they were watching him. He carried on as normal, but kept track of them at the same time.

Once he had everything they needed for the journey ahead, he made his way back to the tavern.

The bartender was wiping down tables when he walked in. Dain made it half-way across the room before the bartender spoke. He didn't want to appear rude, so he stopped where he was and turned back to face the bartender.

"Are you off?"

"Yes, we'll be leaving soon," he said. "Is there a problem?"

Dain knew they needed to be out today, but Taredd hadn't said anything about being out by a certain time.

"Nope, just wondering if you were staying another night, that's all," the bartender said as he moved from one table to the next.

"No, we'll be leaving soon," he confirmed. "So, we won't be needing another night."

The bartender nodded his head. Dain thought that was the end of the conversation, so he continued walking.

Just as he was about to go through the door and head up the stairs, the bartender stopped him again.

"A couple of people were in here earlier asking about the Humans you're with," he said.

"What sort of people?" Dain had a feeling he already

knew the answer, but he had to be certain.

"The sort that likes to drink blood." The bartender looked up at that point. "It's not often we get Vampires around here, and we like it that way. Nasty bastards, all of them."

Dain couldn't agree more. They were all nasty bastards, and that was putting it nicely.

He knew it wouldn't be long before they caught up, but he thought they would have a little more time before they did.

"What did you tell them?" Dain asked.

He kept his voice as calm as he could, even though he was ready to attack at a seconds' notice. He didn't care how kind the bartender had been to them; he would rip his head off if he'd told the Vampires about them.

"I told them that I hadn't seen you," the bartender said, surprising him.

"Thank you," he said.

"Don't thank me," the bartender said. "I was doing it as much for me as I was for you. I don't want or need their kind coming in here and tearing my place apart looking for you. I can't promise that others around here have said the same. So, if I were you, I'd be heading out of town pretty swiftly."

"Thanks for the heads up," he said. "I'll get the others and then we'll be on our way."

"I would recommend taking the Humans out the back when you leave," he said. "Less people will see you that way."

"Thank you again," Dain told him.

The bartender nodded his head before he turned around and continued wiping down the tables.

With nothing left to say, Dain headed up to the bedroom. Taking the stairs two at a time, he was at the top and outside the bedroom door in seconds.

Amberly was sitting on the end of the bed when he walked in the room. Taredd and Natalia were sitting opposite her on the chairs with the table between them.

All three of them stopped talking and turned to look at him as he entered room.

Amberly smiled when she realised it was him. He didn't want her to think there was anything wrong, so he smiled back.

He knew instantly that Taredd could tell something was wrong, but thankfully, he didn't say anything. He just gave Dain a questioning look.

Dain made the slightest movement with his head to indicate that they needed to get going as soon as possible because trouble was on the way. Taredd grimaced in acknowledgment.

"So, what have I missed?" he asked.

He placed the bags with everything he'd collected by the door before walking over to the bed. He kissed Amberly on the forehead before sitting down next to her.

"Not a lot," Taredd said in a tone that meant the opposite. "They were just quizzing me about our realms. They wanted to know what it was like and what the differences were between them."

"We were talking about Taredd's home," Natalia said. "And how nice it was going to be living there."

The thought of Amberly living with Taredd made his blood boil. Even though he knew Taredd had no interest in Amberly, it still didn't ease the sudden burst of jealousy and rage at the thought of her living with another man.

"I'd love to see your home," Amberly told him, instantly calming him at the same time. "From what Taredd's told us, it sounds beautiful. Not to mention, I'd love to listen to the birds singing at night."

It made him smile and warmed his heart that she remembered him telling her about the birds singing at night. "I would love to show you around."

"I would like to visit too," Natalia added.

"And we will," Taredd told her. "But first, let's just get you both safely to my home."

And there was the jealousy and rage again.

"Talking of which," Dain said, trying to change the subject before he launched at Taredd. "It's time to get going."

"What's happened?" Amberly asked, concern lacing her words.

"Nothing," he said innocently. "It's just time we made a move so they can clean the rooms ready for the next guests."

"He's right," Taredd agreed. "Plus, we need to leave while it's still reasonably early so we can get in as many daylight hours as we can."

If it wasn't for Amberly and Natalia, they wouldn't need to stop each night. But the females couldn't go without sleep, and they couldn't sleep in the back of the cart while it was moving, so they had to stop each night.

"Okay," Amberly said, not sounding as if she believed them for one second, but she didn't question them further.

"I'm ready," Natalia said cheerfully as she jumped up from her seat.

"You two wait here while Taredd and I load up the cart," Dain said.

"We can help carry things downstairs," Amberly offered.

"No, it's okay," he assured her. "It'll only take a couple of minutes and then one of us will come back up for you."

"Well, I might as well sit back down again," Natalia said, not seeming bothered at all that she couldn't help.

Amberly on the other hand, seemed like she wanted to argue about it.

"We'll be fine," Natalia told her. "They're only downstairs."

"Okay," Amberly said on a sigh.

Dain was grateful she was going to wait in the bedroom. It meant he had time to talk to Taredd without her overhearing their conversation.

"We won't be long." He kissed her on the forehead before walking out the room with arms laden with bags.

Between him and Taredd, they were able to carry all the bags down to the cart in one go.

"So, what's really going on?" Taredd asked when they were alone.

"Vampires have been in the tavern asking about the

females," Dain said.

"Shit."

"Exactly," he agreed. "We knew they would come after her."

"Yeah, but we didn't think they would catch up so quickly." Taredd shook his head. "What did the bartender tell them?"

"That he hadn't seen us. But that doesn't mean everybody else around here has done the same."

"Do you believe him?"

"Why would he lie?" Dain asked. "What would he have to gain? No, I think he was telling the truth. He didn't have to tell me they'd been asking about them. He could have just kept quiet, or worse, told them where we were."

"True," Taredd agreed.

"So, we need to leave as soon as possible."

As Dain loaded the last of the bags on the back of the cart, Taredd hooked the horse up to the front.

"He also advised that we leave through the back of the tavern with the females."

"Good idea," Taredd agreed. "Less people will see us leaving and the direction we go in."

"My thoughts exactly."

Thankfully, the horse and cart were already out of sight from the main road. So, they didn't need to worry about people seeing them load up the cart ready to leave.

It was easy to take the horse and cart from the stable to the back of the building without being seen, which was why they had kept them there in the first place.

"I'll go get Natalia and Amberly," Taredd said when they were done.

"Okay, I'll meet you out the back."

Dain hadn't brought up the subject of Amberly's eyes glowing because he was still wrapping his head around it himself. He didn't doubt that she was a Shapeshifter. Whether she was a full blood or half blood, he didn't know, but it would explain why they didn't glow all the time like his and other Shapeshifters.

Whether she was full or half blood, she still needed to know about it if she didn't already. And as much as he didn't like it, it was down to him to break the news to her.

He might need to teach her first, but at least she would be able to defend herself against the Vampires when she's able to shift.

That's if she's even able to shift.

If she was a half blood, then there was no guarantee she would be able to shift. She hadn't so far that he knew of.

The only way he was going to know for sure was to ask her. He just didn't know how to start the conversation.

Chapter 23

Natalia did nothing but talk the entire time Taredd and Dain were out of the room. Amberly could tell she was excited to be going to the Demon realm to live with Taredd, and she wanted Amberly to be just as excited as she was.

But she wasn't. If she was being honest, living in the Demon realm seemed more like a nightmare than a dream come true.

Amberly was happy for Natalia, she truly was, but she didn't want to live with them. She didn't want to hurt her feelings either, so she smiled and nodded her head as if she agreed with everything she was talking about.

Thankfully, it wasn't long before Taredd returned to the room to get them. She was a little upset Dain hadn't come up for her, but she refused to let it show.

They followed him down the stairs, but instead of taking them through the main room and out the front door, he quickly ushered out the back of the tavern.

Dain smiled when they walked outside, but she could see he was on edge as he waited for them. He helped her climb on the cart while Taredd helped Natalia, and then both men quickly took their places at the front.

Amberly and Natalia barely had a chance to sit down in the back of the cart before it began moving.

They travelled in silence for most of the day, and at a faster pace than before. Amberly was grateful for the silence, but her arse didn't like the faster pace one bit. Especially since they hadn't stopped as often either.

She had already been suspicious that something was wrong when Dain came back to the tavern that morning. But she was even more suspicious after sneaking out the back of the building and then travelling non-stop for hours.

She didn't know what had spooked Dain at the village, but whatever it was, it wasn't good.

They had put as much distance between them and the village as fast as they could. They were miles away before Taredd finally broke the silence.

"I think we've got another hour, two at most before we have to stop for the night," he told them.

"Good," Natalia said. "Because my arse hurts like hell sitting in the back here. Did we really need to go so fast? I'm sure it made the bumps feel a hundred times worse."

"It's not much better up front," Dain told her.

It didn't help that the road leading away from the village was a lot rougher than the one they had taken on the way there. If it could even be called a road.

It was more like a dirt track littered with rocks and hidden potholes. Not to mention the tree roots sticking up all over the place. It was a wonder the wheels hadn't fallen off the cart, it had been that rough in places.

"We can stop now, if you prefer?" Taredd asked.

"Yes, please," Natalia and Amberly moaned in unison.

Taredd laughed, but Dain stayed silent. He had barely said two words since they left the village. He'd sat in the front of the cart, looking around constantly.

"Could we have something to eat as well?" Natalia asked.

"Of course," Taredd chuckled. "Dain can get a fire started while I find somewhere for the horse to drink."

The river they had stopped by last time had snaked along beside them for most of the day, but it veered off a while back. Amberly wasn't sure if it would join up with them again, but it would be handy if it did.

After sitting on the back of the cart all day, she could quite happily take a dip in the river again.

"I think we should carry on for a little while longer," Dain piped up.

Natalia moaned. "Do we have to?"

Amberly knew exactly how Natalia felt. She didn't want to carry on either.

"Why?" Taredd asked.

"I think the path will join with the river again soon," he said. "If I'm right, it would make more sense to carry on and then camp by the river for the night."

"Okay," Taredd said. "It sounds like a good idea to me. We'll carry on a little while longer."

Natalia moaned again.

"Don't worry," Taredd assured her. "Not for too much longer."

"Thank God," she groaned.

"How are you doing back there?" Dain turned around in his seat to look at Amberly as he asked her.

"I could definitely do with a break," she told him. "But I don't mind waiting a little while longer."

Not that she had any choice in the matter. It wasn't as if she had control over the horse and cart. So if Dain and Taredd didn't want to stop, then they wouldn't.

"You'll get a break soon, I promise." He smiled before turning back around, but it didn't reach his eyes.

It was obvious whatever had bothered him that morning, was still playing on his mind. She wanted to ask what was wrong, but at the same time, she was scared to know the answer.

A few minutes later, she picked up a faint sound of rushing water in the distance. But since neither Dain nor Taredd mentioned it, she kept it to herself.

They must be able to hear it, she thought.

After all, they were the ones with super hearing, not her. So, they should have picked up on it long before she did. Unless they had done and chose not to say anything?

It was possible, but she didn't understand why they would keep it to themselves if they could hear it.

"Well," Taredd eventually said. "It seems like you were right."

"What?" Natalia asked.

"The river's just up ahead," Taredd told her.

"Really? How do you know?"

"Because we can hear it," Dain told her.

Amberly could see Natalia listening intently before she said, "I can't hear a thing."

"That's because you're Human," Taredd said. "We're not close enough for you to hear it yet, but give it a couple of minutes and you'll hear it as well."

They were nearly on top of the river before she excitedly said, "I can hear it now."

Moments after Natalia said she could hear it; the river came in to view.

Taredd didn't pull the horse to a stop straight away. He waited until they came to a clearing before finally stopping.

"Thank God," Natalia said as Taredd helped her down. "Solid ground at last."

Amberly had to agree with her. She was glad they had finally stopped for the night.

It was amazing how tiring sitting in the back of the cart could be. Maybe it was because her body had been tense for most of the journey. Or maybe it was because she hadn't slept much.

Either way, she was absolutely knackered and ready for a break from the cart.

"Thank you," she said to Dain when he helped her down.

"You're welcome." This time the smile he gave her reached his eyes.

Instead of smiling back at him, Amberly hid a yawn behind her hand which made his smile wider.

"Someone's tired," he said.

"I wonder why," she said, grinning at him.

Dain winked at her before turning away to grab a couple of the bags from the back of the cart. Her eyes were glued to his fine arse as he carried them over to a small patch of grass in the centre of a group of trees.

When she finally dragged her eyes off him and looked up, Natalia was staring at her with a massive grin on her face.

"Don't say a word," she mouthed.

Natalia zipped her mouth closed and threw an imaginary key over her shoulder before joining Dain and Taredd as they set up camp.

Dain quickly got a fire going so they could cook dinner, while Taredd dealt with the horse.

Amberly and Natalia wanted to feel useful, so they set up the rest of the camp. By the time they sat down to eat, the sky was turning dark blue and stars were beginning to twinkle.

The moon was almost full. Another night or two and it would begin to disappear again, ready to start another cycle.

It shone down on their campsite, adding a little extra light where the fire didn't reach.

After dinner, she and Natalia turned in for the night. Amberly chose to sleep on the floor by the fire again.

Thankfully, she had a bedroll to help soften the ground this time.

It wasn't as comfortable as the bed she'd slept in the previous night, but it was a lot better than the blankets she used before that.

Natalia's soft snores came from the back of the cart within minutes of her saying goodnight, letting everyone know she was sound asleep. But Amberly couldn't sleep.

Her mind kept going over everything that had happened to her since she made her way through the mountain pass. Bella, the Vampires... Dain. It all raced through her mind as soon as she closed her eyes.

She didn't want Dain and Taredd to know she was still awake. So, she evened out her breathing and pretended to be asleep.

"I've been thinking," Taredd said quietly, finally breaking the silence. "The Vampires probably saw you leave the tavern earlier."

"I know," Dain said softly. "They were watching me when I was walking around the village."

"How do you know?"

"I spotted them not long after I left the three of you," he said.

"Why didn't you say anything?"

"I didn't want them to worry," he admitted.

Amberly had a feeling something was wrong when they left the tavern, and now she knew for certain. The Vampires had caught up with them.

She knew it was only a matter of time before they

did. They made it abundantly clear that she would never escape them. She should have known Dain and Taredd wouldn't be able to keep her away from them forever.

"It's not looking good," Taredd said.

"Yep," Dain sighed. "I don't think we have long before they catch up with us."

"We need to tell them," Taredd said.

"I know."

Silence dragged out between them. Amberly was tempted to turn over to see if they were still there, but she managed to hold herself still.

"So, what do you want to do?" Taredd finally asked.

"I don't think we have any choice," Dain said. "Sooner or later, they're going to catch up. And when they do, they're going to try taking her back. I would rather be ready and waiting for them, than risk getting caught unprepared."

"You want to stay and fight?" Taredd asked, surprise and concern evident in his voice.

"Yes," Dain replied instantly. "I want to stay and fight."

She hadn't been at all surprised that the Vampires were looking for her. But what came out of their mouths next, shocked her to her core.

The conversation between them quickly veered away from the Vampires and onto her.

"It's not going to be easy fighting the Vampires with two Humans to look out for," Taredd admitted.

"Yeah, about that," Dain said. "I don't think we have to worry about two Humans."

"What do you mean?" Taredd sounded confused.

He's not the only one.

"I mean, I don't think they are both Human," Dain said. "I may be wrong, but I don't think Amberly is. Or if she is, she's not fully Human."

Amberly nearly gave away that she was awake and listening to them when Dain had said she wasn't Human.

"If she's not Human, then what is she?" Taredd asked. "And what gives you the impression she isn't?"

Dain was silent for a long time. She was about to jump up and demand he answer Taredd when he finally spoke.

"Her eyes glowed."

"What? When?" Taredd asked, mimicking the words in her head.

"I first noticed it by the river," he said. "I wasn't sure if I was imagining it the first time, that's why I didn't say anything before now."

"But you're certain now?" Taredd asked.

"Yes," he said. "I'm a hundred per cent certain. Her eyes were definitely glowing." There was a brief pause before he added, "They were glowing amber."

My eyes have never glowed, she thought. *And they're not even amber. They're blue, for fuck's sake. No, Dain must have imagined it. There's no other explanation.*

"She's a Shapeshifter?" Taredd sounded just as surprised as she was.

"Or at least, part Shapeshifter," he said.

"Does she know?"

"I don't think so," Dain said. "If she does, she's very good at hiding it."

A Shapeshifter? Me? Amberly thought. *They must be joking. There's no way I'm a Shapeshifter.*

Surely her mother would have told her she was a Shapeshifter if it was true? But she never said anything about her being anything other than Human, which made her think Dain was mistaken.

He must be because I'm not a Shapeshifter, she thought adamantly.

"I would say so," Taredd said. "Especially if she's managed to keep it a secret all of her life."

"So, Natalia hasn't mentioned anything to you?" he asked.

"No, not a word," Taredd said. "As far as she's aware, Amberly's just like her."

That's because I am the same as her! She screamed in her head at them.

"It would also explain why the Vampires kept her alive," Dain said.

"They would think it was their lucky day catching one of your kind," Taredd said.

"Especially if that person doesn't know they're a Shapeshifter," Dain agreed.

Amberly didn't want to hear any more of what they had to say. She would give anything to be asleep right then, so she didn't have to listen to them. But it still eluded her.

Thankfully, they barely spoke after that, but the damage was already done. She couldn't unhear what they had said, but that didn't mean she had to believe it.

Her mother wouldn't have lied to her about something so important. She wouldn't have told her all those stories about how dangerous Shapeshifters were if she knew Amberly was one of them. If her own daughter was one of them.

Unless that was why her mother told her all those stories? To keep her away from their kind so she wouldn't find out that she was one of them?

Amberly hated to think badly about her mother, but it did seem like something she would do. Especially, if it meant keeping Amberly safe.

No! It's not true!

She refused to believe her mother would keep something so important from her. He may be right about the Vampires coming after her, but he was wrong if he thought she was anything other than Human.

The thought of facing off against the Vampires made her blood run cold. At least she wouldn't be alone when she next faced them. Dain and Taredd would be right there with her.

She took comfort in the knowledge that they wouldn't leave her to fight off the Vampires on her own.

When she finally drifted off to sleep, Dain was waiting to greet her in her dreams.

Chapter 24

Dain spent the rest of the night watching Amberly as she slept. He thought long and hard about how to break the news to her she wasn't Human.

It was going to be a lot for her to take in. To find out that she wasn't Human after believing she was for her entire life. It was going to be difficult explaining that without her getting upset or hurt. Neither of which he wanted her to be.

Half the night was spent trying to figure out how he was going to tell her that she was a Shapeshifter. The other half was spent trying to figure out what they were going to do about the Vampires.

Dain stood by what he said to Taredd. There was no point in running because the Vampires would eventually catch up with them.

He would much rather stand and fight. At least that way they could prepare themselves, and the females, for what was to come.

Even though they were out in the open, it would be better to stand their ground than try to run to safety. It was too easy for them to be caught off guard while travelling.

He was just as clueless about how to break it to her when dawn broke and the birds began to sing in the trees, as he was the first time he'd noticed the glowing amber in her eyes. The only thing that had changed was his feelings towards her.

He assumed it was just lust that attracted him to her. She was an incredibly beautiful female, there was no doubt about that. But it was more than just looks.

She had an inner strength that rivalled anyone he had ever known. And even after everything she'd been through, she was still kind-hearted.

He wasn't so sure anymore that it was only down to lust that attracted him. The more time he spent with her, and the closer they became, the more he was beginning to think she was his mate.

The animal side of him had known all along, but the Human part had taken a little longer to catch on. But both sides were now on the same page.

Now all he had to do was convince Amberly that she was meant to be with him. He just hoped she didn't hate him for what he was about to tell her.

"Morning beautiful," Taredd said as Natalia sat up in the back of the cart.

"Morning," came Natalia's sleepy reply.

A moment later, Amberly stirred. She groaned as she stretched out on the bedroll before sitting up.

"Good morning," Dain said to her.

Amberly smiled weakly. "Morning."

From the way she held herself, to the tone of her voice, Dain could tell something was bothering her.

"Did you sleep okay?" he asked, trying to get more than one word out of her.

"Yeah, I suppose." She shrugged her shoulders. "The bedroll is better than nothing, but it isn't as good as the bed back at the tavern."

Some of the tension in his stomach eased, but it didn't disappear completely. She may be talking, but there was definitely something wrong.

She wasn't as cheerful and happy as she usually was. Instead, she seemed more withdrawn. It was like the barriers she had up when they first met had gone back up, but thicker and higher than ever before.

Taredd chuckled. "No, it's not."

"Tell me again why we had to leave the tavern?" Amberly asked.

"Because we need to find our friend Arun," he lied.

He didn't like lying to her, but he didn't want to break the bad news as soon as she opened her eyes either.

She'll know the truth soon enough, he thought.

When the time was right, he was going to tell her everything.

"What's for breakfast?" Natalia asked as she climbed down from the cart and joined them by the fire. "I'm starving."

Taredd laughed. "You're beginning to sound like Dain. Always complaining you're hungry."

"Nothing wrong with having a healthy appetite," she said. "Especially when the food tastes so good. Trust me, if you'd lived on the crap we've eaten all our lives, you'd be constantly hungry as well. Not to mention how small the portions had to be."

"Don't worry, there's plenty of food to keep you happy," Taredd said as he leaned down and brushed his lips with Natalia's.

She smiled up at him. "I think I'll wash up in the river before eating."

"Okay," he said. "I'll make sure your breakfast is waiting for when you're done."

"Thank you," she smiled.

"I think I'll come with you," Amberly said as she climbed to her feet.

"Don't go too far," Dain said.

He wasn't keen on them wondering off on their own. Especially since they knew the Vampires were closing in on them.

"Don't worry," Natalia said. "We won't." She grabbed a few items from the cart before heading towards the river. "Come on, Amberly, let's go."

Dain watched as Amberly followed quietly behind Natalia. When they disappeared from sight, he joined Taredd at the cart and began collecting things for breakfast.

"So, when are you going to tell her?" Taredd asked

quietly.

"After breakfast," he said. "At least by then she would've had a chance to wake up properly."

"Do you really think it's a good idea to leave it so long?" Taredd said. "The Vampires could be here any minute. Do you really want to wait until they are?"

Taredd had a point. It would be better if she knew what was going on before the Vampires arrived. But she already seemed closed off. He didn't want her to withdraw even more.

"You're right," he relented. "I should tell her now."

"What are you going to tell her first?" Taredd asked.

"I honestly don't have a clue." He ran a hand through his hair as he exhaled. "I was up all night thinking about it, and I still don't know where to start or how to break it to her."

It didn't matter what he told her first, neither was going to be particularly good news for her.

He was worried about how she was going to take the news. The last thing they needed was for her to run off on her own while the Vampires were looking for her, and that was a possible outcome.

"Well, rather you than me," Taredd said.

"Thanks," Dain said sarcastically. "Sure you don't want to swap places?"

Taredd burst out laughing before walking away.

Yeah, thought not, Dain thought. *Lucky me.*

He always seemed to draw the short end of the stick, but with Amberly, he wanted to be the one to tell her that she was a Shapeshifter. He just hoped she didn't take it too badly.

If she did, he didn't know what he was going to do. He couldn't change what she was, and neither could she. But no matter what, he would be there for her.

He wanted to be the one to show her how to be a Shapeshifter, and teach her everything there was to know about their kind. But first, he needed to tell her.

Not wanting to put it off any longer, he dropped what he was doing and headed towards the river.

"Just tell Natalia I need her help," Taredd told him.

"I will do," he said over his shoulder.

He could hear Natalia talking the entire way to the river. He'd come to realise she was definitely the talkative one out of the two of them. Amberly mostly nodded along with her, barely saying a word.

"Hey, Dain," Natalia said when she noticed he was walking towards them. "I thought you were staying with Taredd? Is everything alright?"

"Everything is fine," he told her. "Taredd has just asked if you'll give him a hand with something."

"Yeah, of course," she said, then turned to look at Amberly. "You'll be okay by yourself for a minute, won't you?"

"Yeah, I'll be fine," Amberly told her.

"Don't worry, I'll stay with Amberly," he told them.

"Okay, cool," Natalia said. "Be right back."

Before either of them could say a word, Natalia skipped back to the campsite.

"Couldn't you have helped Taredd?" she asked after a moment.

"To be completely honest, he doesn't need any help," he confessed. "I needed to speak to you, and I think it's better if we talk in private."

The look on her face spoke louder than any words.

"I'm not," she blurted.

"Not what?"

"I'm not a Shapeshifter."

He had a feeling she was pretending to be asleep when he'd spoken to Taredd about her. In hindsight, he should have waited until he was certain she was asleep, but he'd wanted to get it out in the open.

"I heard you talking to Taredd," she confirmed. "You told him that I'm a Shapeshifter. It's not true. I'm just a Human."

Dain took a deep breath and exhaled it. "I know it's hard to believe, but it's true, you are a Shapeshifter. Or at least, a half-blood."

"What? Because you thought you saw my eyes glow, that makes me a Shapeshifter?" she asked.

"I didn't think I saw them glow," he told her. "I know I saw them."

"Then why have I never seen it happen?"

"Unless you've looked at yourself in a mirror as you orgasm, you wouldn't have seen them," he said bluntly.

Amberly jolted back as if she'd just been struck across the face.

He inched closer to her as he softened his voice. "I'm sorry, Amberly, I should have found a better way to tell you. I didn't mean for you to overhear me telling Taredd. I know I should have spoken to you before I

254

told anyone else."

"You must be wrong," she said adamantly. "My mum would have told me if I was a Shapeshifter."

"Was your mum Human?" he asked.

"Yes!" she snapped. "If she wasn't, she wouldn't have warned me to stay away from your kind."

"What about your father?" he asked.

"I... I don't know," she stuttered. "My mum never spoke about him. He died before I was born."

"Is it possible he was a Shapeshifter, and that's why your mother warned you to stay away from us?" he asked.

Amberly was silent as she thought about his question. She looked so lost and alone as she paced in front of him. So scared.

Dain wanted to pull her into his arms and tell her everything was going to be fine. But until they dealt with the threat from the Vampires, he couldn't make that promise.

He hadn't even brought up the subject of the Vampires yet. He was dreading her reaction to that news.

He could just imagine what they put her through, knowing full well what she was. And he bet they didn't enlighten her for fear of what she would do with that knowledge.

"I want to say no," she finally said. "But the truth is, I just don't know. She never spoke of him. Every time I tried to bring him up, she would change the subject. So, it's possible he could have been a Shapeshifter."

Dain could understand why her mother hadn't told her

about her father. It was possible that one of his kind had raped her mother, and that was why she hadn't wanted to talk about him.

"If I am one, then why can't I shift into an animal?" she asked.

"I'm not sure," he told her.

"And why hasn't anyone else seen my eyes glow?" she asked. "You're not the first person I've slept with, but none of my past lovers have mentioned it."

He knew she wasn't a virgin, but he still didn't like the thought of her being with anyone other than him.

"I wasn't sure if I was seeing things the first time," he admitted. "It was just a quick glimpse. It was only when I told you to hold eye contact the last time that I knew for definite."

"That still doesn't explain it," she said. "I've held eye contact with others as well."

"Maybe it's because I'm a Shapeshifter and your past lovers were all Human." Even speaking the words left a bad taste in his mouth.

"That's the only thing it could be," she said. "Because they were definitely Human."

There was no guarantee her eyes would have glowed if she'd slept with another Shapeshifter. There was no way he was going to let her test the theory either. He would rip any male Shapeshifter to shreds that even thought about going near her.

Mine! He thought possessively.

It wasn't the only explanation as to why it only happened with him. It could also be because she was his mate, but he didn't think she was ready to hear that just yet, so he kept it to himself.

Chapter 25

Amberly hadn't been able to stop thinking about what she'd overheard the night before. It was the first thing that entered her mind as soon as she woke up that morning.

She didn't want to believe her mother had kept it a secret for all of her life. But Dain was right, she didn't know anything about her father, so it was possible he was a Shapeshifter.

Her mother had refused to talk about him. Every time Amberly tried to bring him up, she would quickly change the subject.

Amberly wished she could be alone for a little while so she could think about everything, but Dain wouldn't have it. He told her it wasn't safe enough for her to be on her own.

He did relent and leave her by the river with Natalia. Even then, Taredd had to convince him that they would be fine before he finally left them alone.

Dain and Taredd would still be able to hear if anything happened while they were at the river. So, she wasn't concerned.

Since Dain hadn't brought up the Vampires when he'd spoken to her about being a Shapeshifter, she assumed they weren't as close as he originally thought. If they were, surely it would have been more important to speak to her about them instead of discussing whether or not she was a Shapeshifter.

"Is everything okay with you?" Natalia asked.

She was surprised Taredd hadn't told Natalia what was going on. He seemed to be leaving it for Amberly to tell her when she was ready, and she was grateful for that.

She was still wrapping her own head around it; she didn't need to be trying to explain it to Natalia at the same time.

"Yes, why?"

"You seem quiet this morning," she said. "I know you've been a lot quieter since, you know, since everything that happened to you. But I thought you were starting to be you again."

"I am me," Amberly told her. "That's one thing that hasn't changed."

It didn't matter whether she was Human or a Shapeshifter, deep down she was still the same person she had always been. Maybe a little more broken with a few more scars, but she was still the same.

"You know what I mean," Natalia persisted. "I know you've been through a lot, and that's why you've been quieter than normal. But before we left the tavern, you were talking… asking questions… even laughing… and it was like having the old you back. Then this morning, you seem distant again."

"Sorry," Amberly said. "I just have a lot on my mind, that's all. I promise, nothing is wrong with me."

"Good," Natalia smiled. "You would tell me if there was though, wouldn't you?"

"Of course," Amberly lied. "You'd be the first to know."

Amberly hated lying to Natalia, but until she could wrap her mind around it, she didn't need her asking questions she didn't know the answer to.

Natalia looked at her questioningly for a moment, but thankfully, she didn't ask any more questions.

Instead, she wrapped her arms around Amberly's neck and held on tight.

"I'm so happy you're still with me," Natalia said softly. "I thought I'd lost you."

"I'm not going anywhere, I promise," Amberly assured her. "So, you better get used to having me around because I'm gonna be bugging the shit out of you for years to come."

She tried lightening the mood, but it didn't work. Natalia held her even tighter.

"You best not be going anywhere," Natalia's voice broke as she fought to hold back the tears. "I'll hunt you down if you do."

Hugging Natalia back just as tightly, Amberly said, "I'm not, don't worry."

Finally letting go, Natalia wiped away the tears that had escaped. She turned towards the river and instantly froze.

Amberly turned around to see what Natalia was looking at and came face to face with the Vampires. She looked back towards the campsite, ready to run at a second's notice, only to see they were behind her as well.

"Shit," she breathed.

Dain had been right. The Vampires had been on their trail all along, and now they had finally caught up with them.

While they had been talking, the Vampires had quietly surrounded them, cutting them off from Dain and Taredd. She heard Taredd swear followed by an all mighty roar seconds before fighting broke out behind her.

Natalia grabbed hold of Amberly's hand and squeezed it tight. Amberly gently squeezed her hand back, trying to reassure her that they would be alright.

She could hear Dain and Taredd fighting their way over to them, so all they had to do was hold on until they could get there. Amberly was sure they could do that. She'd give it a bloody good try anyway because there was no way she was going with the Vampires again, and she certainly wasn't going quietly.

It didn't matter if she was a Shapeshifter or not, she

would fight to the death if it came to it.

"Well, well, well, what do we have here?" one of the Vampires sneered at them. "Looks like the filthy animal that thought she could get away."

"I'm no animal," she sneered right back. "You are."

"You really don't know, do you?" he laughed. "No, my sweet treat, you are the only animal here."

So they know as well?

She filed that bit of information away for later. She really wanted to ask if her eyes had glowed when they had raped her, but she held back. For all she knew, they could have figured it out by drinking her blood.

If that was the case, she really didn't want to bring up them raping her. She didn't even want those memories floating around in her head, let alone adding to the visuals that kept popping up by speaking about it.

"What do you want?" Natalia demanded.

"Isn't it obvious?" he continued to stare at Amberly as he replied to Natalia. "I've come to take back what is mine." He finally tore his eyes away from Amberly and looked at Natalia. "You'll do nicely for a snack." He tilted his head as he inspected her. "But I don't think you're going to be quite as tasty."

"We're not going with you," Amberly said, snapping his attention back on her. "We will fight you."

She may not have stood a chance against them last time they faced off because it had been a handful of Humans against a horde of Vampires. But it was different now.

Now she had back-up in the form of Dain and Taredd,

a Shapeshifter and a Demon. She could still hear them fighting in the background as they tried to make their way to her and Natalia. As long as she could hear them, she knew there was still hope.

The circle of Vampires burst out laughing at her words.

"You don't have a choice in the matter," he told her. "If you think the Demon or that other animal will stop us, then you are mistaken."

He nodded at somebody behind her, and before she had a chance to react, two rough hands clamped down hard on her shoulders. Out of the corner of her eye, she noticed Natalia jump, letting her know that she had been grabbed as well.

Amberly growled. The strange sound vibrated through her throat. She didn't know who was more surprised by the animalistic sound coming from her, Natalia or the Vampires. But she was just as shocked as the rest of them.

It was one thing to think she might be more than Human; it was another to actually hear the proof of it.

Natalia's head swung in her direction as her mouth dropped open. As much as Amberly wanted to tell her everything, now was definitely not the time. So, she ignored Natalia and kept her eyes on the Vampire in front of her.

"We are not going with you," she repeated.

The Vampire moved so fast, that within the blink of an eye, he was stood in front of her with his hand raised.

Her head snapped to the side and pain explode through

her cheek as his hand made contact with her face. Then his hand was on her again. This time he grabbed her by the chin and made her look up at him.

She tried to pull away, but the Vampire holding her from behind stopped her.

"You have no choice!" Saliva flew out of his mouth as he shouted in her face.

A second later, Natalia screamed as she pushed to the ground. One Vampire held her down while another tied her wrists and ankles together. She tried to fight against her captor, but she didn't stand a chance against them.

I can't watch another friend died!

As soon as the thought left her mind, everything turned black, and she was transported to the safe space inside herself. The place where the Vampires couldn't reach her.

No! She screamed in frustration.

She couldn't watch another friend die, but that didn't mean she wanted to be trapped inside her own mind while it happened either. She wanted to fight back, to show them that she wasn't going with them, and neither was Natalia, but she couldn't do that from the safety of her mind.

Unlike her previous visits to the dark recesses of her mind, this time Amberly wasn't alone. A giant cat with black and white strips greeted her.

Its long tail swished back and forth as it prowled towards her. As frightening as the creature appeared to be, she wasn't scared of it. Somehow, she knew it wasn't there to hurt her, only to bring her comfort.

She stood in place as circled around her, rubbing its body against her at the same time. She couldn't stop herself from reaching out to touch the beautiful animal.

Half expecting it to move away, she was surprised when it nuzzled its head into her hand and purred. Warmth spread through her along with the vibration from the sound.

Amberly gently scratched it behind the ears and was rewarded with a lick on the arm before it turned and walked away.

Instead of curling up into a ball like she would normally do, she took a deep breath and followed the animal into the darkness. Unafraid of what was to come, she knew whatever happened, she wouldn't be alone.

Chapter 26

He had known the Vampires were coming after her and that it was only a matter of time before they caught up, but he hadn't expected it to be so soon. He honestly thought they would have more time to prepare. That he would have more time.

He was glad Amberly and Natalia had listened to him and stayed close by, but there was still a big enough gap him and the part of the river where they were. The Vampires had taken full advantage of the gap. Cutting off him and Taredd so they had no choice but to fight their way through.

Dain was more than willing to fight them to get to Amberly. He didn't care how many were between him and Amberly, he would take them all on by himself if he had to.

Thankfully, he wasn't alone. Taredd was just as eager to reach Natalia as he was with Amberly.

Luckily, they were still together, so it made his and Taredd's job a lot easier. It just needed to stay that way until they got there.

Their chances would be a hell of a lot better if Arun was with them, but he wasn't. So they had no choice but to deal with them on their own.

Taredd swore at the same time as Dain shifted into a Siberian Tiger. He tilted his head up to the sky and let out an almighty roar before he leapt towards the Vampires.

Even prepared as they were, the Vampires still weren't ready for him. He pounced on the closest one, knocking the Vampire onto his back. Using his teeth and claws, Dain ripped him to shreds within seconds. As soon as the Vampire was dead, he moved on to the next one.

Taredd was just as quick with his first kill, but then the Vampires seemed to snap out of their trance and leapt into action as well.

He was just about to bite down on a Vampire's throat when he was suddenly yanked off and sent flying through the air. Pain shot through his chest and the wind was knocked out of his lungs as he hit a tree.

He landed in a heap on the floor. It only took him a second or two to get his breath back, but while he was lying on the ground, the smell of singed fur reached his nostrils.

Alerted to the fact his tail was on fire, he quickly whipped it through the air, extinguishing the flames as quickly as they had started.

Fuck!

The Vampire that threw him had followed him over to where he landed. Just as he was about to grab Dain's tail, he spun around and clamped his teeth down hard on the Vampire's leg.

Screaming in pain, the Vampire tried to pull away, but that just cause him more pain because Dain had a solid grip. He didn't let go until the Vampire fell over backwards, landing straight on top of the fire.

The Vampire instantly caught on fire. He squirmed around, trying to put out the fire, but it was too late for him. He wouldn't make it to the river even if he managed to get to his feet.

Dain didn't spare the Vampire a second thought. He was straight back on his feet and racing over to the fight in the next heartbeat.

Taredd was dropping bodies left, right, and centre, but he was still no closer to Amberly and Natalia than he was when he started.

Dain quickly joined in the fight. Swiping at their legs with his razor-sharp claws, he waited until they fell to their knees before finishing them off.

Blood drenched his fur, and bits of flesh stuck between his teeth and claws as one Vampire after another blocked his way.

He didn't know how Amberly and Natalia were holding up. Knowing they were alone with the Vampires filled him with a fear he'd never felt before.

There had been few times over the years he'd been

afraid, so he wasn't used to the feeling. But the fear he felt for Amberly was like nothing he'd ever experienced before, and he didn't like it one bit.

It was made worse when Natalia's scream echoed all around them. Taredd was going ballistic at the sound, and Dain couldn't blame him.

As hard as they fought, they weren't making any headway. They needed to come up with a new plan otherwise they were going to lose Amberly and Natalia, possibly for the rest of their lives.

No! Dain snapped.

He would die before he let the Vampires take Amberly away from him, and he wasn't prepared to die just yet. He planned on spending many happy years with Amberly before that day came.

Quickly looking around him for a way past the Vampires, it didn't take long for an idea to form in his head. If he couldn't go through them, he would go over them instead.

Dain smiled, which looked more like a snarl coming from the tiger's face.

Before the Vampires knew what he had planned, he raced towards the closest tree and leapt fifteen feet into the air. Landing gracefully on a thick branch, he worked his way through the canopy towards the river.

Why he hadn't thought about doing that earlier, he didn't know. Maybe it was the worry and fear for Amberly's life that had clouded his mind from seeing a way through, or maybe it was the surprise of being quickly surrounded by Vampires. Either way, he didn't care.

What mattered most was that he was able to close the distance between him and Amberly.

Taredd was still fighting his way through by the time Dain reached the river. As he took stock of the situation below him, his blood began to boil, and his vision turned red.

Natalia was pinned to the floor by two Vampires as they tied her wrists and ankles together. They were about to do the same to Amberly, but suddenly jump back away from her when she shifted into a majestic white tiger.

The beautiful black and white strips rippled as she shook out her fur for the first time.

I knew it! He thought happily as he looked down at the magnificent creature.

He'd been right all along. She was a Shapeshifter, but he still didn't understand why that part of her had never come forth before. Why didn't it show itself when she was first attacked by the Vampires? Why had it waited until now?

Dain didn't have the answer, and probably never would. He was just glad it had finally come forward to aid her when she needed it.

Tail twitching, she crouched down and snarled at the Vampires around her. Like a cornered animal, she was ready to defend herself in an instant.

He heard Natalia sucked in a breath as she looked at Amberly in complete shock and awe. Amberly's head snapped towards Natalia as she heard the sound as well.

There was absolutely no warning before Amberly

pounced. Knocking both of the Vampires off of Natalia in one fell swoop as she lay helpless on the ground.

Taredd roared when he heard Natalia scream for a second time. Thankfully, her scream was more from surprise than because the Vampires were harming her.

Dain didn't bother looking back at where Taredd was still fighting his way through the Vampires. He could hear the commotion.

The Vampire that had been stood in front of Amberly before she shifted into a tiger, tried sneaking up behind her as she tore into the two she had knocked off Natalia. It was then that Dain snapped back into action.

Pushing away from the tree at the same time as jumping down, he hit the back of the Vampire. The Vampire stumbled forward, tripping over Natalia's legs before regaining his balance.

Amberly spun around ready to attack, but stopped short when she noticed him. He chuffed at her, letting her know it was him and that he meant her no harm.

She chuffed back before turning her attention on the Vampire he'd knocked. She gave no warning as she pounced on him.

This time the Vampire wasn't able to regain his balance. He toppled backward, landing flat on his back next to Natalia's feet.

He didn't stand a chance against Amberly. Before he was able to more an inch, she was on top of him. He screamed out as her claws pierced his skin, but was quickly silenced when she bit down on his neck.

Dain made sure no other Vampires tried sneaking up

on her while she was distracted. When she released the dead Vampire from her grip, she turned towards the rest of them.

Amberly and Dain took up position on either side of Natalia and faced off against the Vampires as a team. She was still lying helpless on the ground, and Taredd was still fighting his way over to them, so it was down to them to keep her safe.

After seeing their leader and two of their comrades being taken down within seconds of each other, the rest of the Vampires quickly scattered without so much as a backwards glance.

Dain was positive it wouldn't be the last they would saw of the Vampires, but at least he knew Amberly was able to defend herself against them now that she could shift. And more importantly, they knew she could shift to defend herself.

Taredd immediately raced over to Natalia and untied her wrists from behind her back. He helped her sit up before removing the restraints from around her ankles.

Natalia rubbed her wrists. Bruises were already beginning to appear from where she had tried to get free from the rope.

Pulling her into his arms, Taredd held on to her tightly.

"Are you okay?" he asked as he frantically checked her over for injuries.

"I'm okay," she assured him. "Amberly saved me."

When she turned to Amberly, she had adoration and wonder in her eyes.

"I… I never knew…" she said as she reached out to

touch Amberly.

Thankfully, Taredd stopped her before she made contact with Amberly.

When she looked up at him questioningly, he said; "She's not thinking straight at the moment but give her time."

Dain could see sadness in her eyes as she looked back at Amberly.

Still in Tiger form, she continued to look around them for the Vampires. She paid absolutely no attention to Natalia, Taredd, or himself. She was solely focused on where the next attack was coming from.

"Dain," Taredd said.

He didn't hesitate to shift back into Human form. "It's okay, I've got her. Take Natalia back to the campsite and we'll join you there in a minute."

"Are you sure?" Taredd asked.

"Yes."

With the way Amberly was acting, it was safer for Taredd to take Natalia back to the campsite and leave him to deal with her. She wouldn't purposely attack Natalia, but with how on edge she was, all it would take is a simple touch for her to snap.

As Taredd led her away, he heard Natalia ask, "Is she going to be okay?"

"Yes," Taredd assured her. "Dain knows what he's doing. He'll have her back to normal in no time."

When they were alone, he held out his hands as he slowly approached Amberly to show her that he meant no harm. With it being her first time shifting, and still being in attack mode, he wasn't sure how she was going to react. So, he needed to be cautious and ready for anything.

Thankfully, Amberly let him approach her without a problem. She even let him stroke the silky soft fur on top of her head.

He couldn't take his eyes off her. She was absolutely stunning in animal form, the most beautiful white tiger he'd ever seen. But it was now time for her to shift back.

The danger had gone, at least for the time being. So, she didn't need to stay as in tiger form any longer.

She stared up at him with those glowing amber eyes in full display. The sadness and confusion he saw swimming in her beautiful big eyes made his chest constrict.

Crouching down in front of her so they were eye level, he spoke softly as he assured her they were safe. "You can shift back now. You're safe, I promise."

Amberly gently shook her head as she pleaded for his help as she looked at him. He instantly understood what was wrong. She didn't know how to turn back into her Human form.

Dain gave her a comforting smile as he told her what to do. "Just close your eyes, take a deep breath, and picture yourself as a Human again."

She did as he said and closed her eyes, but it took her a couple of minutes before anything happened. Dain waited patiently, stroking her head to let her know that he was still with her, and that she was safe. And then it happened.

In the blink of an eye, she shifted back. One second

she was on all fours in front of him, and covered from head to tail in black and white stripy fur. In the next, she stood on two unsteady feet, completely naked.

"Thank you," she whispered before passing out.

Dain quickly reached out and caught her before she could hit the floor.

"Amberly?" he gently shook her as he called her name.

But she didn't respond to him. Not even an eyelid twitched as she lay limp in his arms.

Holding her tightly against him, he stood up and carried her unconscious form back to the campsite where Taredd and Natalia were waiting for them. He didn't say a word as he walked past them towards the cart, and thankfully, neither of them tried to stop him.

Once he reached the cart, he gently placed her down on the bedroll and then covered her over with a blanket.

"Is she going to be okay?" Natalia asked, worry evident in her voice.

"Yes, she'll be fine," he told her. "She's just exhausted herself out from shifting. She just needs some rest and then she'll be back to normal in no time."

"I hope so," Natalia said.

He turned around and looked at their destroyed campsite. The ground was littered with dead bodies.

Taredd had moved some of them to the side, but it made little difference. The last thing he wanted, was for Amberly to wake up and see the damage left behind by the fight. He didn't want it to be the first thing on her mind either, but he had no control over that.

"I think we should go back to the tavern," he said. "I don't want Amberly waking up here and seeing all this."

"I agree," Taredd said. "I think it would be a wise decision to go back to the tavern for the time being. At least until she'd had time to recover."

"I'm definitely up for going back," Natalia added.

"She might wake up along the way, though," Taredd pointed out.

"Yes, I know," he said. "But at least she won't have to see all this."

After the amount of energy she'd just expelled, she was going to be out cold for a while. He had a feeling it could be days before she finally comes to.

Either way, at least she wouldn't have to look at all the dead bodies as soon as she opened her eyes.

Chapter 27

No matter how hard she tried to fight it, she couldn't stop herself from waking up.

As she began to stir, imagines of her dream flashed in her mind. It was the weirdest dream she'd ever had in her entire life.

She had imagined that she'd turned into a giant cat with black and white strips covering her entire body, right down to the tip of her tail. Amberly was amazed her mind could conjure up such a majestic creature when she had never seen one in real life.

She'd seen a few pictures of black and yellow cats before, but she couldn't remember what they were called.

She was also fighting with Vampires in her dream. Shredding them to pieces with razor-sharp claws the size of large knives and ripping their throats out using nothing but her teeth.

The dream was so realistic, Amberly swore she could taste their rancid blood in her mouth as she woke up. The sound of their bones cracking under her massive paws as her claws sliced through their skin still rang in her ears.

"Amberly?" someone called to her.

At first, she didn't recognize the voice saying her name. It was only when it came a second time that she knew who was calling her. It was Natalia.

"Amberly?"

"Just a little while longer," she groaned. "I don't want to get up yet."

The bed was so incredibly comfortable, she really wasn't ready to leave it just yet.

In her dream, they had left the tavern in search of Dain and Taredd's friend. She was glad to find out that wasn't the case because that's when all the trouble started in her dream.

First with Dain insisting she was a Shapeshifter like him and making her think her mother had lied to her about it. And then later on with the Vampires attacking them.

"You've been sleeping for two days straight," Natalia said laughed. "How much more sleep do you need?"

That certainly woke her up. Her eyes snapped open, but that was the only thing that moved. The rest of her body felt like a lead weight.

"What?" she gasped.

"You've been asleep for two days," Natalia repeated.

"How much more sleep do you need?"

"What the fuck?"

No matter how tired she'd been in the past, she'd never slept for such a long period of time before. There must have been a reason, she just couldn't think of one.

"What happened?" she asked, hoping Natalia could tell her.

"We were attacked by the Vampires," Natalia said. "But you saved us."

The dream came flashing back into her mind. Well, what she thought had been a dream and was now turning out to be real.

"How?" she asked, confused.

How the hell was she able to save them from the Vampires? Unless, she hadn't been dreaming about turning into a Shapeshifter all along. She had actually turned into one in real life.

"It was real."

"It was definitely real," Natalia confirmed. "I got to see you shift up close and personal. You should have seen it, Amberly, you were absolutely amazing. After you turned into a tiger and killed three of the Vampires, the rest of them ran away with their tail between their legs."

Natalia laughed, but Amberly didn't find the funny side of it.

"Not literally," Taredd said. "Because they don't have tails."

Natalia waved away his words. "Tish, tosh. They still ran away from her."

"Yes, they did," he agreed. "It was a sight to see."

Amberly didn't know what surprised her more. The fact she'd scared off the Vampires, or how proud Taredd and Natalia seemed to be of her.

When she sat up and looked around the room, her heart sank a little when she noticed Dain wasn't there.

"He'll be back soon," Natalia told her.

"Where's he gone?" she didn't want to seem desperate, but she needed to see him, to make sure he was okay.

"Just downstairs to get you something to eat," Taredd told her. "He had a feeling you would be waking up soon. He was hoping to be here for when you did, but he must have been held up downstairs."

As the last word left his mouth, the bedroom door swung open and Dain strolled in.

Amberly's heart skipped a beat when she saw him. He was even more handsome than she remembered, but she could tell he was tired. Even from a distance, she could see the dark circles under his eyes.

"You're awake?" he said when he spotted her sitting up on the bed.

"Yes," she said.

"She's just woken up," Natalia told him. "So, you were right."

"How are you feeling?" he asked as he walked over to her.

"I'm okay," she said. "Just a little tired."

"Still?" Natalia asked in surprise.

"That's to be expected," he said. "You expelled a

lot of energy." He looked between Taredd and Natalia before continuing. "Do you know what happened?"

"They were just telling me about the Vampires and that I turned into an animal?" she half said and half asked at the same time because she still couldn't quite believe it.

"That's right," he confirmed.

Amberly was silent as she mulled over everything they had told her.

"It's getting late," Taredd said after a moment. "So, we'll let Dain fill in the rest and we'll see you both in the morning."

Natalia leaned down and gave Amberly a quick hug.

"See in you the morning," she said when she stood back up.

"Yes, see you in the morning," Amberly smiled at Natalia as she turned and walked away.

Taredd followed her out of the room and closed the door behind them.

"Are you sure you're okay?" Dain asked as he perched on the side of the bed.

"Yes, I'm fine," she said. "I'm just a little confused."

"Tell me what's confusing you," he said. "I might be able to help."

Amberly took a deep breath before she began. "Natalia said I turned into a tiger?"

"Yes," he said. "You shifted into a beautiful, majestic white tiger."

"So that's what the black and white cat was," she said, thinking out loud. "Did you shift as well? I mean, when the Vampires surrounded us?"

"Yes, I shifted into a tiger like you, just a different colour," he told her.

"How come we both turned into the same animal?" she asked.

"I'm not sure," he admitted. "I knew which animal would be best suited to fight in that situation, that's why I picked a tiger. It could be that the Shapeshifter part of you instinctively thought the same thing, and that's why you shifted into a tiger as well. They are deadly creatures in a fight, and very nimble."

"Is that why you turned into one?" she asked.

"Yes."

Amberly was silent as she let that bit of information sink in.

"I don't know anything about my father," she finally said. "My mother told me he died before I was born, and that Shapeshifters were to blame. She said they killed him while he was out collecting supplies. That's why she drummed it into me to stay away from them. From you. She told me you were all evil and would kill me too if you ever caught me."

"Do you feel the same way as your mother did?" he asked. "Do you think we are all evil?"

Even though he didn't give away any hint of emotion, she could tell he wasn't happy. She knew her next words had the potential to push him away, and that was the last thing she wanted.

"No," she said. "I used to, but not anymore."

"What changed?" he asked.

"You did," she said. "You changed me, my mind, everything. Before you rescued me, I thought exactly the same way as her, but you changed that. You didn't have to go out of your way to rescue me, you could have told Natalia that you didn't see me. And then you tended to my wounds. You were so kind and gentle; you were nothing like my mother made you out to be."

"I would have done the same for anyone," he said.

"Maybe," she agreed. "But it still doesn't change the fact you did those things for me."

"Is that why you had sex with me by the river?" he asked. "Because I was kind to you?"

"No," she said. "I don't know what came over me at the river, I've never been so bold in my life." When he looked at the floor, she added, "but I don't regret what we did. I'm glad it happened."

"I don't either," he said as he looked back up at her.

Desire now darkened his eyes where before there was nothing, but that wasn't the only thing she saw. Hope and love were also there for her to see.

"Amberly, I have to ask you something," he said, looking worried again.

"Okay," she dragged out the word, unsure if she wanted to know what the question was.

He gently took hold of her hands and looked into her eyes before asking, "Will you be my mate?"

Amberly was taken aback. She hadn't been expecting him to ask her that, she didn't know what to say.

"You don't have to answer straight away," he said. "I understand if you need time to think about it. Speak to

Natalia first, if you need to."

She pulled one of her hands out from under his and placed a finger on his lips.

"I don't need to think about it," she said. "I already know the answer."

She had always known the answer, even if she didn't know the question. She was meant to be with him, meant to spend the rest of her life with him. She didn't need to think about something that felt so right.

Deep down, she had known all along that she was his mate. She just needed him to ask the question.

Amberly threw her arms around his neck and held him tight.

"Yes!" she said excitedly. "The answer is, yes."

Dain leaned back and looked at her for a moment.

"Really?" he asked, surprise clear in his voice.

"Yes," she nodded.

Dain smashed his mouth against hers in a kiss filled with passion as he frantically undressed her. Amberly was just as frantic as she tried to pull his clothes off, but she ended up ripping them off him instead.

"Sorry," she murmured against his lips when the button to his trousers pinged off somewhere across the room.

Dain broke the kiss as he said, "Don't worry about it. I have plenty more clothes."

Amberly couldn't help but giggle when she looked at how dishevelled he looked. Strands of fabric hung off him in long strips, and she hadn't only popped the button off his trousers, she'd nearly ripped them in two.

"Well," he said as he looked down at the remains of his clothes and then at her discarded nightshirt. "At least I managed to get your clothes off in one piece,"

He stood up next to the bed to remove the remnants of his clothing.

When he was done, he gently pushed against her shoulder until she was lying on her back. Then he wrapped his hands around her ankles and lifted her feet off the bed.

Amberly automatically bent her knees as Dain lifted her legs up higher.

"That's it," he said. "Now, hook your arms under your knees and hold them up for me."

She did as he asked, hooking her arms under her knees. When she was ready, he let go of her ankles and gently pushed her knees further apart.

Amberly felt extremely exposed in that position, but the desire she saw in his eyes as he looked at her, gave her the confidence to widen her legs further still.

Goosebumps raced over her body as he slowly ran his hands up the inside of her thighs to her core and then used his thumbs to spread her open.

"You're already wet for me," he said huskily as he gazed down at her exposed flesh.

Amberly sucked in a breath when she felt his thumbs dip inside her. He coated them in her juices before running one after the other over the bundle of nerves, eliciting a moan from her.

His eyes flicked to her face before returning to watch what his thumbs were doing. When he dipped his thumbs inside her again, she felt him press against the sides.

"Look at that beautiful pussy," he groaned. "So hot and wet for me. So open for me."

Dain slid one of his thumbs out of her and began rubbing it against the bundle of nerves. At the same time, he slowly pushed his other thumb in and out of her.

As she started to relax, her legs fell open even further until they were nearly touching the sheets.

"That's it," he said huskily. "Relax for me, baby. Let me see all of you."

Still rubbing the bundle of nerves with one thumb, he swapped the other for two of his fingers. Pressing them inside her before spreading them apart as he pulled them back out.

Over and over again, he repeated the movement until she was tensing up like a tightly coiled spring and begging for more.

"Soon," he told her as he continued playing with her. "Just keep your legs open for me, baby."

A second later, he pushed in a third finger and twirled them around inside her before pulling them out. Amberly nearly came there and then, but she bit down on her lip to hold it back.

He repeated the movement several more times, pushing slightly harder and faster each time he entered her.

Amberly's arms and legs began to shake from holding them open for so long. Dain must have noticed as well because the next minute he was positioning himself between her legs so his face was level with her core.

He tapped her hands and said, "Let go."

She instantly did as he told her and let go of her legs. When her hands were out of the way, he hooked her feet over his shoulders and then wrapped his arms around her thighs and spread her open with his fingers.

"You smell so good," he groaned. "I need to taste you."

Before Amberly could make a sound, Dain's lips were on her. Kissing from one leg to the other and back again. It was torture feeling him so close to her core, yet never touching her there.

She was ready to scream at him to do something, anything, when his tongue finally flicked across the bundle of nerves. Amberly jolted at the touch. If Dain hadn't been holding her down, she would have pulled away.

Stretching her arms above her head, she pushed against the headboard as he showed her no mercy as he devoured her.

He flicked his tongue over the sensitive nerves and then sucked on them before gently scrapping his teeth against them. As much as she was enjoyed it, she needed more.

Dain must have read her mind because a moment later, he was pushing his fingers inside her again. Stretching her as he pushed them as far inside her as they would go before pulling them out.

Again and again, he pumped his fingers in and out of her, winding her tighter and tighter. He was moving slowly at first, but soon built up speed until he was pounding his fingers inside her.

Amberly couldn't take anymore. She couldn't hold back the orgasm anymore. Her head pressed into the pillow as her back arched with wave after wave hitting her.

Chapter 28

Time seemed to stand still while he waited for Amberly to answer his question. He told her she could have time to think about it and that she didn't need to answer straight away, but deep down, he needed to know.

When she said yes, his heart had felt like it was going to explode, he was so happy. There was no way he could put of mating with her any longer. It had been hard enough waiting for her to wake up so he could ask her.

Many times over the two days that she'd been asleep, Dain had wanted to shake her to see if that would wake her up. The only reason he held back was because he knew she needed the rest after the energy she'd expelled from shifting for the first time.

If it hadn't been for that, he would have done anything

in his power to wake her up sooner. To see her lying beneath him completely naked as he pleasured her body.

Dain could watch her all day, every day, and not tire of seeing her orgasm. He would never tire of seeing the way her back arched, pushing her ample breasts up as an offering whenever she tipped over the edge.

He couldn't get enough of her. He was still licking the juices from her as she finally stopped convulsing around his fingers.

"Mmm… you taste so good," he groaned.

Amberly moaned as more moisture coated his fingers.

He pumped them inside her a couple more times before pulling them out completely. He licked the juices from them and then crawled up the bed.

When he was eye level with her, she pushed against his shoulder until he was lying on his back and then she straddled his waist. She gave him a seductive grin as she crawled backwards so she straddled his thighs instead.

Her warm hand wrapped around his rock hard cock, making it twitch. Slowly, she worked his length up and down several times before leaning down and taking the head into her mouth.

She swirled her tongue around the tip, coating him in her saliva before sliding him further into her mouth. When she couldn't take anymore of him, she squeezed his cock between her tongue and the roof of her mouth before sliding his cock out again.

She repeated the move, taking more of him inside her each time, but she was still unable to take all of him.

So, she wrapped one of her hands around his shaft and slowly stroked up and down his length in time with her mouth.

Dain was enthralled as he watched his cock disappear between her plump rosy lips. His hands fisted at his sides to stop from grabbing hold of her hair. He knew she wouldn't want him touching her there while she was sucking his cock, so he did his best not to.

Cupping his balls, she gently massaged them with her free hand. He nearly shot his load there and then. It took all of his willpower not to thrust, especially when she took more of him into her mouth.

His blood was on fire as she sent waves of pleasure racing through his body. Dain had to bite his lip to stop from coming when he hit the back of her throat and she started to swallow his cock, taking him further inside her than she'd ever been able to before.

When she repeated the move, he lost all control. Shouting her name to the ceiling as come shot down her throat.

She didn't stop swallowing his cock until she'd drained him dry. Then, as his cock slid free from her mouth, she licked the sensitive tip.

Amberly sat up with a confident smile on her face. She licked her lips before crawling up the bed again.

Dain could feel the heat from her pussy as she hovered above his cock. He desperately wanted to grab her by the hips and slam her down, impaling her on his cock at the same time, but he held back. The last thing he wanted to do was hurt her.

Instead, he waited patiently as she lined up his cock with her entrance. As she slowly lowered herself on to him, he bit his lip and forced himself not to move.

Dain held her hips to help steady her as she took all of him inside her. She was so hot and wet that his cock slid easily inside her, but it still took her several tries before she was able to take all of him.

Amberly closed her eyes and arched her back when she was fully seated. She looked incredibly sexy in that position.

Dain couldn't resist running his hands up her body. He followed her curves until he reached her breasts. Cupping one in each hand, he rubbed his thumbs over her pert nipples.

Amberly leaned forward, pushing her breasts into his hands as she rested hers on his chest. Using his chest to help steady her, she began to lift herself up until only the tip of his cock remained inside her. She hovered like that for a second before lowering herself down again.

She moved slowly at first, but it wasn't long before she found her rhythm and began to build up speed.

As she bounced up and down on his cock, her breasts bounced with her. Dain massaged them in between playing with her nipples. Amberly sucked in a breath every time he ran his fingers over their sensitive tips.

When she started to slow down, he quickly sat up and sucked one of her nipples into his mouth. He alternated between her breasts, sucking and nipping the tips of her nipples as she slowly bounced up and down on his cock.

Needing to take back control, he let go of her breasts

and grabbed her waist. Amberly didn't get a chance to complain when he lifted her off his cock and spun them around.

As soon as she was on her back, he was wedging himself between her legs. Without warning, he lined up his cock with her entrance and then thrust all the way inside her in one swift motion.

She gasped at the sudden movement, but it soon turned into a moan of pleasure.

Her back arched, pushing her breasts up like an offering. Dain didn't refuse. He leaned down and sucked one of the tight buds into his mouth.

Amberly's fingers ran through his hair as she held him against her. He gave her a minute to adjust to the new position before he started moving inside her.

He planned to take it slow, but as soon as she was underneath him and he began to move, he couldn't stop himself from pounding inside her. Amberly didn't complain as his cock slammed in and out of her. She met him thrust for thrust with pleasure filled cries for more, and he gave it to her.

Dain could feel his balls tightening as he came closer to the edge. Thankfully, she was right there with him.

This time, when the urge to mate with her hit him, he didn't hold back. He took her mouth in a fiery kiss as his fangs lengthened in his mouth in preparation for marking her as his. He could feel her fangs doing the same.

Unable to hold back any longer, he broke away from her mouth to trail kisses down her neck to her shoulder.

He gently licked the soft skin between her neck and shoulder and felt Amberly do the same to him.

Just as they tipped over the edge into the sweet abyss of ecstasy, they bit down, piercing each other's skin and entwining their lives forever as mates.

Epologue

For the first time in Amberly's life, she felt like she had a future to look forward to. A future filled with love and laughter, and lots of adventures. A future with Dain by her side.

She couldn't deny it any longer. She was a Shape-shifter. Not only had she seen the glowing amber in her eyes, but she had also shifted into a white tiger twice.

The first time was still like a dream. She remembered bits and pieces, but it was as if she was watching it rather than being a part of it. So, she shifted the day after waking up from her long sleep.

After hearing Natalia talk about how beautiful the animal was, she was eager to see it for herself. With help from Dain and Taredd, she was able to see herself in a mirror.

They were right, the tiger was a magnificent creature. Its thick fur was covered in black and white strips, from the tip of its nose, all the way down to the tip of its tail. She still couldn't quite believe it was her, even though she'd seen it with her own eyes.

Amberly kept half expecting to wake up at any moment to find out it had all been a dream and that she was still in the Vampire camp.

Nothing was ever going to be the same, and she was happy with that. She still missed Donovan and always would. She wished he could have lived to see a better future, but at least he wasn't scared or suffering anymore.

He wasn't having to constantly hide in bunkers or run for his life. So, as much as she missed him, she knew he was in a better place.

Everything looked different to her now, like the world wasn't as scary a place as she thought it was all her life. She didn't know if it was because she'd found out she was a Shapeshifter, or if she was just seeing things in a new light.

But as she looked down at the street below, she didn't see creatures to be scared of anymore. She saw creatures like her, just trying to live life to the fullest.

Amberly knew it wasn't as black and white as that. She knew there were still creatures out there that were dangerous, but there were also a lot of kind-hearted creatures as well.

Dain and Taredd were prime examples, they had the biggest hearts she'd ever seen. They just needed a little push to do the right thing from time to time. Even the tavern owner was one of the good guys.

"You okay?" Dain whispered in her ear as he walked up behind her and wrapped his arms around her waist.

She turned in his arms and looked up into his beautiful amber eyes and nodded.

"More than okay," she said. "I'm feeling better than I've ever felt before."

That wasn't a lie. She didn't know if it was because she was a Shapeshifter, or part Shapeshifter, but she hadn't felt so good in her life.

Some of the reason why she felt so good was definitely because of him. He made her feel safe, confident... loved.

He was about to say something to her when there was a knock on the door.

"That'll be Taredd and Natalia," he said.

Amberly groaned. "Do we really have to leave now? Can't we stay for one more night?"

They had already stayed for a week so she could fully recover before they hit the road again, but she still wasn't ready to leave. She could happily spend the rest of her life locked away in the bedroom with Dain, but she knew it couldn't be.

They needed to find their friend and then get Natalia back to Taredd's home in the Demon realm because it still wasn't safe for her to be in the Human realm.

It wasn't so bad for Amberly in the Human realm anymore. Now that she wasn't Human, or completely Human anyway, it wasn't as dangerous for her. Especially since she'd proven she could take care of herself, but it wasn't the same for Natalia.

"I suppose you're right," she said.

He kissed her on the forehead before releasing his grip. Amberly's arms dropped to her sides as she watched him walk away.

"Are you two ready yet?" Taredd asked as soon as Dain opened the door.

"We'll be ready in a minute," he said. "I've just got a few more things to pack up. So, you might as well come in and wait."

"I thought we both agreed to leave at this time," Taredd said. "So, I thought you would have been ready to go."

"Stop bitching," Dain said. "It won't take me long."

"I don't mind waiting," Natalia said as she walked past him. "Amberly and I will just chat while we're waiting."

Taredd reluctantly followed her inside the room, closing the door behind them.

"I suppose a few more minutes won't hurt," Taredd relented.

"Nope, it won't," Dain agreed.

Amberly sat on the bed with Natalia while Dain gathered up their last few belongings. Taredd was about to take a seat at the table when the bedroom door was suddenly thrown open, making everyone in the room jump.

Instantly on guard, Dain and Taredd spun around ready to attack the intruder, but stopped short when they saw who it was.

"Arun?" they said in unison when a man with long white hair stepped through the door.

"What are you doing here?" Dain asked.

"We were about to go looking for you," Taredd said.

Arun looked around at everyone in the room before turning back to Taredd and Dain.

"I need your help."

To Be Continued…

Dear reader

I hope you enjoyed reading this book as much as I enjoyed writing it.
Please could you take a moment to leave a review, even if it's only a line or two, about what you thought of the book.
Also, if you'd like to know about upcoming new releases, sneak-peeks, and special offers you can sign up to my newsletter. You can also find me on Facebook, Bookbub, and Goodreads.
Thank you and much love.

Georgina.

www.georginastancer.co.uk
www.facebook.com/AuthorGeorginaStancer
www.bookbub.com/profile/georgina-stancer
www.goodreads.com/author/show/18724439.Georgina_Stancer

Guarded by Night series

Kissed by Stardust
Connor's New Wolf
Midnight Unchained
Darkest Bane
Hidden Demons (coming soon)

Infernal Hearts series

Heart of the Hunted
Heart of the Damned
Heart of the Cursed

Heart of the
Cursed

Prologue

A shiver raced down Selene's spine as she entered an abandoned library.

No matter how many dilapidated buildings she searched through, she would never get used to the creepy vibe they gave off. Every time she entered one of them, a shiver ran through her.

Even though she was alone, she could never shake the feeling of being watched. She half expected someone to jump out at her at any moment. Selene hoped that never happened, but she was prepared, just in case.

Dark and dingy didn't even begin to describe the state of the rundown building. She'd seen pictures in history books of what some of the buildings had been like after the last human war, but it was nothing compared to the state of them now.

Centuries worth of dirt and debris had been blown inside, coating every surface in a thick layer of grime. The remains of the doors were little more than firewood, and not a single window had survived.

The shattered glass crunched under her feet as she made her way around the room. It was mixed with bits of broken slate that at one time would have been used to cover the roof.

From the look of the place, the roof had caved in years ago. Everything in the main room was destroyed. Books were scattered on the floor, along with a mountain of rubble and whatever nature had blown in through the broken doors and windows, and water dripped from the gaping hole where the ceiling used to be.

Selene hoped the book she was looking for wasn't in the main room. If it was then the Human race was well and truly fucked.

No! She refused to believe that. She refused to believe Humans was beyond saving.

After hundreds of years of being mercilessly hunted down and killed, the Human race was nearly extinct. And it all started over a war the humans had played no part in. It was a war between the supernatural creatures from all the realms, not just the human realm.

Most of the creatures the humans had only read about in books. They thought they were only stories to scare and entertain. They hadn't known the monsters were real until the war started.

She could just imagine the shock and horror at coming face to face with one of the creatures for the first time. After thinking they were nothing more than a made-up story, it must have been quite the surprise.

Selene wasn't old enough to remember the war, but her mother had told her about it. She had told her about all the creatures because she had wanted Selene to be prepared for when she would come face to face with them. It was never a matter of if, but when she would cross paths with them.

Her heart ached at the memory of her mother. She was a kind-hearted soul that would have helped anyone, human or not.

As much as her mother tried to keep the monsters at bay, she had known the day would come when Selene would have to face them. Unfortunately, that day had come when Selene was far too young.

She remembered that day all too well. It had been burned into her memory. Not only was it the first time she would see the monsters, but it was also the last time she would see her mother alive.

Selene shook her head. She didn't want to think about the past. Especially not that part of her past. She would much rather remember the good times with her mother. Though, it was becoming more and more difficult to remember those times.

It had been many years since her mother had

died, and with each year that past, it became harder to remember her. The way she looked, the sound of her voice, it was all a distant memory that was fading away with time.

Concentrating on the task at hand, she surveyed the area around her. Everything in the main room had been destroyed. It would take weeks to check every book in the room.

Selene would spend the time looking, if she thought the book was there, but she didn't think it would be.

From what she knew of humans from before the war, it wasn't the type of book that would have been on display with the rest. Since it was the only one of its kind, it would have been kept somewhere safe. Somewhere out of sight from prying eyes.

She would have kept it in a safe place, concealed by magic. But humans didn't have magic. At least, none that she'd come across. So, they had a tendency to lock it away in a thick metal box. Some were small, no bigger than a shoe box, and others were massive. She had even seen some that were bigger than a library.

Most had been raided years ago, the valuable items stolen. There were a few that she'd come across that were still locked, but she was able to get into them easily enough.

There were a few creatures that could use magic *and* appeared to be human. Selene had crossed paths with plenty of them over the years, plus, she was one of them. She may look fully human, but she wasn't. She had magic of her own.

Her mother had been fully human, she hadn't had a drop of magic in her. So, Selene had inherited all her magic from her father, whoever he was.

She'd never met him, and the couple of times she'd asked her mother about him, all colour had drained from her face and she'd quickly changed the subject. That was all the answer Selene needed to know that he wasn't a good person, and she was to stay well away from him.

Selene hadn't told her mother about her magic. After the way she'd reacted when Selene had asked about her father, she thought it best that her mother didn't know what she could do.

She couldn't bear the thought of seeing fear in her mother's eyes whenever she looked at her, which would have likely been the outcome if she'd ever found out. So, Selene kept her abilities to herself.

She was making her way around the room when something off to her right caught her eye. She backtracked a step and squinted as she peered into a dark room.

She couldn't make out what it was, but there was definitely something in there. She picked up a broken chair and moved it out of the way before combating a table that was wedged in the doorway.

After several attempts to move the table the human way, Selene finally gave in. She took a couple of steps back before throwing her hands out in front of her and blasting the thing to pieces with her magic.

Bits of broken wood and metal flew all over the place as a dust cloud billowed out of the room.

She dusted off her clothes and waved her hands in front of her face to chase away the dust particles.

"That's better," she said when she saw the doorway was clear.

She was still learning to use her magic. Unfortunate, there was no one around that she could turn to for advice when it came to magic. Even if she could have talked to her mother about it, her mother wouldn't have had a clue what to do.

So, with no one she could turn to, Selene had to figure it all out on her own. It wasn't impossible to do on her own, but it did make it more difficult.

Thankfully, with a lot a practice, she'd been able to gain some sort of control over her magic. In the past, if she'd tried to blast a table out of the way, she could have just as easily blown up the entire building, with her in it.

As soon as the dust settled in the room, Selene stepped inside. She could barely see her hand in front of her face. So, she turned to magic once again.

Selene held her hand up and clicked her fingers. An orb of light instantly appeared above her hand. With a twist of her wrist, she sent the orb flying around the room until it found what she was looking for.

There, in the back corner of the room, was a door to a secure room. The thick metal door was exactly what she'd been looking for. It was the sort of room Selene would have kept the book in if it had been in her possession.

She clambered across the rubble and tried the handle to the door. The door was locked, just as she knew it would be.

Selene wasn't deterred. She pressed her hand against the cold metal and sent her magic into the door to unlock it. She couldn't hear the clicking as the locks opened one by one, but she could feel it through her hand thanks to her magic. As soon as the last lock clicked open, she called her magic back to her and then opened the door.

The safe room was even darker inside than the room she was in. The light coming from the small orb did little to show her inside. So, she clicked her fingers again and produced a bigger orb. She sent the larger of the orbs into the room and kept the smaller one with her.

Other than a little bit of dust, the room was immaculate. Row upon row of shelves greeted her inside, stacked floor to ceiling with books. Each one had a turn-wheel at the end, so the shelves could be easily moved, and each had different letters on them. Not a single book was out of place.

Selene didn't know the name of the book she

was looking for, so she had no choice but to start at the beginning and work her way along. She had a rough idea of what she was looking when it came to the contents, but she would have to look inside each book to rule them out.

It was time consuming, but she had to do it. It was the only way she could help the Human race.

One by one, Selene searched each row of books and came up empty. She was about to give up when she spotted a small, leather-bound book tucked away right at the back of the last shelf.

She gently picked it up and looked at the cover. The only marking was a dragon eating its own tail. Selene knew the symbol was known as an Ouroboros. She'd come across it in another book she'd found.

She ran her fingers over the worn leather and traced the Ouroboros before opening the book. The book was definitely old enough to be the one she was looking for, but after flicking through a few pages, it became clear it wasn't the one.

It wasn't a total loss. The little book contained several spells Selene hadn't seen before. But best of all, there was a small piece of paper sticking out the spine of the book with a locating spell written on it. If nothing else, that would come in handy. So, she decided it was worth taking home with her.

Selene closed the book and placed it in her bag before retracing her steps back to the main room.

Night-time had descended while she'd been in the room, so she kept the orbs with her as she searched the rest of the building.

Even though she doubted the book she was looking for would be kept anywhere else, she checked all of the room. Making sure to check every corner of the place before leaving because she had no plans on returning, ever.

By the time she was finished, the sun was just starting to rise the following morning. With one last look at the library, Selene began the long trek home.

She hadn't found what she was looking for, but she wasn't giving up. If she had to, she would search for eternity. Because after being hunted for so many years, the Human race deserved the chance to live in peace.

The story continues in the final book in the series, Heart of the Cursed.

https://books2read.com/HeartoftheCursed